An Evening of Romantic Lovemaking

Ben Slotky

AN EVENING OF ROMANTIC LOVEMAKING

DALKEY ARCHIVE PRESS

Dallas / Dublin

Library of Congress Cataloging-in-Publication Data Available Upon
Request

Paperback: 9781628974010
EBook: 9781628974270

www.dalkeyarchive.com
Dallas/Dublin

Table of Contents

An Evening of
Romantic Lovemaking

Chapter One

Here's The Part Where I Came In

It's funny, it is, and is everybody back? Back from the bathroom or wherever? Oh my goodness, we've got everybody here, present and I'm guessing accounted for? Good, because I'm only going to do this once, and I'm sorry about that up there, that thing with the picture, I'm not sure what that was, something went wrong. How many do we have here, tonight? [Looks out, counts.] Not a *big* crowd, it doesn't look like not a *big* one. Not *too* surprising. [Slowly clasps hands in front of his chest.] Like seven? That's who's here, is that right, and who'm I asking? [Shrugs, laughs.] Folks, and I'm sorry, and we'll get started in just a sec, I promise. Some technical difficulties, it looks like, nothing to, right, nothing to worry, nothing to worry about. And it's nice here, you know? Down here? On stage? I never stand here, I don't. [A quick, sad smile.]

3

Wow, this is nice and here we are. Brighter up here than I thought. I can't see anything. [Hands shielding eyes, looking out. Tiny smile, quick.] There's so much, so much stuff to *get* to, and okay before we get back to it, maybe a little bit about *me*? [Clasps hands.] Don't worry, we'll get back to whatever it was we were doing but no, but a little bit about *me*, I have six children, I'm *married*, and yeah, I built this place, this place right here. Did it a few years back, renovated the whole, and thank you, that's very kind. [Smiles, quick, fake bow.] This is mine, this is, this *was*, and you probably knew that already. May have seen or heard, and this is good, this is great, this is hands clasping. [Clasps hand, paces.] This is pacing and I *think?*

I think tonight we're going to answer a lot of questions. [Looks out, quizzically.] What's that, ma'am? You didn't *ask* any questions?

[Laughs.] That's good, that is. I mean, you bring up a good point, even though you didn't. [Pacing, walking across stage.] But no, I think a lot of questions are going to be answered tonight, I declare, at least I hope they are. And I know, and I know what they say about hope. [Stops, looks out.] They say hope in one hand and shit in the other: see which one fills up faster. [Scrunches up face, gives quizzical look.]

What was that?

Who says *that?*

Who said that? [Looking out, surprised.]

Great question, ma'am. *They* say that. *They* do. My grandmother said that; we'll talk about her later. We have plenty of time, so *much* time, plenty of grandma time. I say that now, about hoping and shitting, ma'am, and I stopped, didn't I? I'm yeah, now I'm talking about something else, aren't I? But, no, I do, I say it to my kids, except I say crap or poop instead. That's the only difference between what she said and what I say and am saying now. [Pauses. Looks around admiringly, nodding.] And I'm scrambling here, I am, I'll admit it. I have no idea how much time I've got before the cops come, because they almost have to, don't they? Ma'am?

[Tilts head, leans in.] Don't the cops come in a situation like this? Don't they have to, sir? When you take hostages? [Quick shake of head.] Don't the cops always come when shit like this happens? A hostage situation, an evening of romantic what again? [Rubs stomach, paces.]

I read a lot of cop stories, lots of detective stories, ma'am. They always come. The cops do. [Smiles, walks.] You know what'd be fun, ma'am? Writing a detective story. Just a really detailed, really intricate plot, but accessible, you know? Like you get it, you're never lost. Wouldn't that be great ma'am? [Slowly shakes head, small smile.] I'd love to write a detective story, a crime story, and that's a little bit about me, I guess, but not really. I can't do it, though. I've tried. There are plots and pacing and red herrings McGuffins and none of it, ma'am, I'm good at none of it, and this may be pointless right now, I get that. It may be pointless like a new pencil, but how am I supposed to know, you know? I'm just getting this all out there, all of it. I'm declaring, and in those detective stories that I read, ma'am? Those detective stories that I read but cannot write? Sometimes they call the lieutenants "Lou." [Stops, smiles.] Think about that for a second. "Lou." I love that. I love it so much, and I can't tell you why, not really. I can't answer that, I don't know what the words are. [Looks around.] They've got to be here somewhere. Like if it was the answer to a really hard crossword puzzle? Like if I'm supposed to be able to know how to describe that feeling of how I feel when I read about people calling lieutenants Lou. That may or may not be important, may or may not be something I'm going to need to account for later on, I don't know, I don't know. But you know what I *do* know, ma'am? What I can guarantee, sir, what I can goddam *declare*? It's funny, this whole thing is. We're going to have, oh gosh, we're going to have a good time, and I kind of laughed right there, just a little, because it's true, it's true, we are. Don't worry, seriously. You'll be fine, we all will be. We're going to laugh and laugh, but before we *do* that, I just want to lay some ground rules, like on what we're going to see, and I could pretend that there was something wrong with the film, right ma'am? With the projector? From before? Like I could pretend like,

"Oh, you all came in to see a movie and you sat down and started watching and then there was like some technical difficulty, a glitch, a screw up? The film melted or the bulb burnt out or something and *that's* why I'm down here talking now?" This could be the plot, this could be the narrative structure or whatever, but that's not what we're doing, here, is it? And you kind of knew that already, didn't you? [Smiles, tries to wink.] Naw, we're not doing that, we're going to get, it's going to get *deep*.

We're going to answer the big questions.

And it's not *all* going to be serious stuff, don't be alarmed, it's fun, it's an evening of romantic lovemaking.

I saw that look on your face, sir, you were like, "What's all this about deep questions or whatever the fuck? I thought this was about lovemaking? That's what the sign out there says." No, you're right, you're right, and it does, it says so right there, truth in advertising and what have you. [Still pacing.] It's not going to *all* be serious, but we're going to answer some big questions. For example, how did we get here? [Stops, waves hands around.] What are we doing, what are we talking about and what does any of this have to do with otters? [Squints eyes, scrunches face like reading a sign at a distance.] That question, these questions will be answered.

What happens after you lose everything and everything leaves you? [Shrugs shoulders.] What does that *sound* like, how does that *feel*?

[Stops, smiles.] Ma'am, I can *answer* that question, like I can answer that *question*. [Smiles, exhales. Wipes brow with hand.] It's exciting, right?

How do you tie all *that* in with an otter? An otter, ma'am, can you make *that* fit? *Can* you?

Can I get out of here?

Will I be killed?

These are all questions, ma'am, that I *promise* you, I promise you, we'll get into. And I know. [Stops, looks down, shakes head, dejected.] I know what you're thinking. [Smiles.] I know that a lot of comedians are going to come, they're gonna be like, "We're going to talk about these things," you know, and they *skirt around* them, they boot-and-capri-pants-around these issues, I know that. And what's that, now? [Hand to ear, head cocked.]

What're we doing, now?

A comedian?

Well, yeah, I mean, I guess that's what this is going to be. This makes sense. [Paces.] I was a lot of things before, and now I'm this, I guess. Let's check off things I've been, shall we? [Looks out at audience, shields eyes with a hand holding a gun.] Who's up for a little checking things off? An off-checking, an accounting, a declaration? [Shrugs.] Okay, let's see, I've been a *businessman*, right? An entrepreneur, which is fun to say, right? Check. That didn't pan out too well. [Leans in, stage whispers.] 'Bankruptcy! Ssshh!' [Stands back up.] I've been a *husband*, right? A father? A good person who does things husbands and fathers do? Check. [Leans back in, shakes head, purses lips, stage whispers.] "That didn't work out too well. I am totally alone, ma'am. There's nobody here." [Stands back up, shakes it off. Centers himself.] No, but like I've *tried all that*, I've been all those things, and this is where it's led me? [Looks around, surprised.] *Here?* No, but I've been over this a bunch, and I think I am going to frame it like this. Now that it's all over, I'm going to act like I'm a comedian, right?

Why not?

Have fun!

Lovemaking!

And it's one night only, and it's one last time, so we'll give it a shot, right? I've always wanted to do it, to give it a shot. [Waves gun in air, smiles.] And if it's not going to be tonight, then when the hell is it going to be, you know? My then-wife used to always tell me how fucking funny I think I am. [Pauses, leans in.] And the only reason I *knew this*, ma'am, is because she would always say things like "You think you're so fucking funny, don't you?" Things like that, subtle things, sir, hints and tips. Allusions, and whatnot. She'd say things. "This is fucking funny to you, isn't it?" Stuff like that, ma'am. And these are little hints, little tricks. Things I have picked up because I'm very perceptive, right? Attention to detail, ma'am! Everything counts, sir, everything fits and let's do it! [Claps hands.] This is *it*, this is it, and I *know* it. If it hasn't already happened yet, then it's about to, same thing. [Closes eyes, rubs head.] Listen, it's not, I'm not, I know, I know. I wrote a list, ma'am, about things that I know. It's true, I have it. [Pulls papers from pocket.] A whole list, ma'am, a whole list, so [Reading.] so, it *looks like where we are* is I say I guess what I'm going for here is just to tell you that we're going to have fun, yes. [Nods quickly, puts papers back in pocket.] Yes and yes and Okay and yes, *but* and here's where the but comes in, *but* there's also a lot of work to be done here. There was a lot of stuff done to get things to where they are now and now that it's ending, there's a lot more stuff to do. A lot of work. Only problem is, I'm not a hundred percent sure I know what that stuff is, and ma'am? Did you notice that I said *ah* hundred instead of *one* hundred? Did you see that, and by see I mean hear? What that is, ma'am, is attention to detail, ma'am, that's what I do, that's what I've done. Look around this place, look how beautiful it is. And I hear what you're saying, I hear it, I do. You're like, "Where was all that attention to detail when your business was failing." And sir? You're like, "Where was all that attention when your wife was falling out of love with you and you were losing your family?" And to that I can only say "ouch," ma'am. Ouch, sir. Ouch and how dare you. [Shakes head slowly side to side.] But that's not what we're here for, so I'm not going to pay any attention, and

I pronounce attention ah-teyn-shun for some reason. I can't explain it, I can't. The Who couldn't explain things either ma'am, and even though I hate The Who, that's got to be something, even if it probably isn't. So that there, that's a little bit about me, ma'am, and we'll get more later, but yeah, that's a little bit about me. [Stops as if recalling.] I never got into The Who. My friend who looks Jewish but isn't likes the song "Magic Bus," I think, but that's not what this is. We're flailing here, but maybe that's part of it, and here's what I mean. I mean, I'm not sure what I'm supposed to be doing, now that this is over, now that this is ending.

Now that this is ending? No idea. I am supposed to declare bankruptcy, did you know that? Tomorrow, I am.

Did you know that?

Ma'am?

How would you, really?

How would you possibly know that? You're not here for *that*, you're here for lovemaking, am I right? A romantic evening thereof? [Sighs. Sips water.]

Do you know anything about knuckleballs, ma'am?

Do you know anything about segues?

About things tying and tied together? Tied up like a noose, like a knot, like a shanks head or a sheepshank. What were we saying? Knuckleballs? [Eyes wide, surprised.] And I'm not, this isn't, I mean I know how this sounds.

I said knuckle and balls.

I said ma'am. No, this is a real thing, a knuckleball is a real thing. It's a pitch and it's tough to hit. It shifts and it shakes and it looks like it shouldn't go, like it looks out of place around all the fastballs and the sliders and the curves. Those look like they belong. Bam, down the middle, right?

Ninety miles an hour!

Ninety-eight miles per hour!

And why couldn't I hit that?

It was going a hundred miles an hour, that's [Through clenched teeth] why! But then there's a knuckleball and it goes like fifty-eight miles an hour.

It doesn't spin.

It moves around.

It looks like you should be able to smash that thing.

I am a professional baseball player. [Points microphone out at audience.]

This is *you* talking, sir.

You are talking.

You are a professional baseball player, you play baseball professionally. You can hit this thing. [Smiling.]

You can hit what's coming.

It's easy.

Take a swing.

And that was pretty good, right? Ma'am? It was, and I get it, I get it. This isn't what you thought you were here for. This doesn't, right, seem like lovemaking. An evening of romantic lovemaking. That's what the sign says outside. Neon. Bright and flashing. So let's get to it, folks! Who's ready to have a good time? [Looks out, grinning, clapping hands quietly together.]

Folks, thank you very much for that smattering of applause. That's, yeah, that's a very adequate amount, it's accurate, it is. For what you're about to receive. [Smirks, smiles, paces. Holding microphone with right hand, pointing out to crowd with left.] Let's level-set here, let's course-correct. Ma'am, a little bit about *me*? I am forty-six years old. [Tilts head at crowd.] I know, I know. I've said that, I've said this. I'm forty-six, I look great, thank you, ma'am. That is a preemptive thank-you. Like you don't even have to *say* it, you know? It's like I know you that well already. It's amazing, isn't it? How good I look, and I'm forty-six, I'm *married*, I have six kids.

Yeah.

I do.

I have six, six boys. Oldest is seventeen, youngest are twins, they're two. Two years old, ma'am, is what those two are right there. How about it, right? [Looks knowingly at crowd, nods head.] We'll get into it, we will, but a little bit about *me*, I live in Bloomington. That's right, right here. I *do* own this place, this place right here. For like six, seven more hours. That's right. [Holds hands out. Looks up and around.] Built it, renovated it, did all that, did all this. So, I did this, built this. [Stops mid-stride. Pause. Looks out. No applause.]

Huh.

Kind of thought there'd be something there.

A clap, a woo-hoo? Nothing? [Purses lips, nods head.]

That's about right, that's about right. [Continues pacing, head down.] I live in Bloomington, I work here in Bloomington, and a little bit about *me*? Like one thing I *do*? Like if somebody tells me they're from a city. Like I ask and they say they're from Cincinnati. [Looks into crowd.] Like ma'am, say you're from Cincinnati. Like I'll go where're you from and you go I'm from Cincinnati.

Where're you from, ma'am?

[Looks out, eyes wide. Pauses. Nods head.]

Oh really? How many people live there? *That's the first thing I'll say!* Every time! I don't know why. I'm very interested in how many people live in places. [Looks up toward ceiling. Quizzical look on face.]

Oh, you're from Des Moines? How many people live there?

[Looks back at crowd.]

And what am I going to do with that, you know? Like what am I going to do with how many people live in Des Moines? Why is this so important, ma'am? Why is this the first thing, always the first thing? But I can't not do it, I can't. [Pacing.] Like I don't care what you *do*, for a living, I don't, but for some *reason*, I want to know how many people live in a town. Can't explain it, ma'am, won't even try to. So that's a little bit about me, that's me establishing rapport. Something else about me is [Scratches head, rubs stomach] what else, what else? [Looks out at crowd.] Because I feel as if we should, you know, get to know each other better, right? Things being what they are and all?

So you know how sometimes there's a jar of jellybeans? You know how sometimes there's a [Pauses, looks intently at audience] ma'am, *you* know!

You've seen *jars*, right?

You're familiar with *jars*.

You know what a jellybean is. So imagine if you will a jar full of jellybeans, like imagine it. [Clasps hands together, tilts head, wide-eyed.] Just *imagine* it! [Looks back out at crowd, crouches down, looks side to side.] That was a quick impression right there—me doing a guy who was really excited about the prospect of imagining a jar full of jellybeans, folks. That's what that was. To clarify. [Blinks quickly, stands back up, continues pacing.] A jar full of jellybeans? We see it, we've got it, and then imagine somebody comes up to me and goes, "Hey, how many jellybeans do you think are in that jar?" And I'd go, "I don't know, I don't know" or something like that. And they'd go, "Do you think there's like *sixty-five jellybeans* in that jar?" And I'd look and go, "Yeah, about sixty-five jellybeans, that sounds about right." You know I'd look at the jar, I'd gauge it, right? I'd do some jellybean-gauging, some jar-gauging and I'd be like, "Okay, yeah, about sixty-five, about sixty-five." [Nods head up and down assuredly.] And then they'd say something like "Or do you think there's like *seven hundred and fifty jellybeans* in there? Does that sound right?" And I'd pause and I'd look again and I'd go, "Yeah . . . yeah, there's probably about seven hundred and fifty of them." You know, so that's a little bit about me, is that I'm not a good judge about how many jellybeans would be in a jar, what else? Uh, a little bit about *me*, I don't know if I'm an *orgy guy*. [Quick scrunch of the face, shake of head.] You know what I mean, I mean I don't think I'm a, let me clarify, I just don't think I'd do it. And I've been thinking about this a while, if I was an orgy guy or not, because I *assumed* that I was, you know what I mean? [Looks out at crowd.] Fellas? You know? Like if somebody were to say, "Hey, would you like to go into an orgy?" Like theoretically, a hypothetical orgy. [Pauses. Laughs.] And you know, me saying that somebody would say, "Would you like to go *into* an orgy," like that's how that would go, that's the way you'd get invited to an orgy, that kind of shows how not an orgy guy I am, doesn't it? "Say fella, how's about going into this swell orgy we've got here!" Anyway, but no, seriously, let's say I'm invited to a hypothetical orgy, would I go? And I'd like to think I'd be like, "Yeah, I'll go," you know? Like I'd think about it, I'd ruminate for a second.

I'd gauge, I'd orgy-gauge. [Pauses, confused and amused look on face.] And there's been a lot of gauging already, hasn't there? By my count, it's like two types of gauging, jellybean and orgy, and what this has to do with an evening of romantic lovemaking I have yet to determine, but we'll have to muddle through, I guess, but anyway, yeah, like *previously*? Previously, I'd be like yeah, I'll go into the orgy, you know, but now I think no, no way, you know? No way would I go, nothing about it sounds good to me. I don't think I'd do that, go to an orgy. And that's a big deal, you know? Because you go through life and you think something is one thing and then it turns out to be another thing. You know how that is? [Shakes head. Squints eyes and squeezes bridge of nose. Exhales loudly.] And I know, and I know how this sounds, it sounds silly. You're like oh, this is jellybeans and orgies, that's what this is. A goof, a lark. A hoo-haw. [Looks mock-sternly out at crowd.]

Ma'am, are you here thinking this is a hoo-haw? Like a good old-fashioned hoo-haw? I can't see you out there, so I'm assuming. I'm surmising, I'm theorizing, I'm terrorizing, and while I'm doing *that*? While I'm doing that, I want to assure you that this isn't. A hoo-haw, I mean. I'm not. This is serious. This is a declaration. I am confessing, here. These are things I am sharing, little bits of things.

Jellybean things, orgy things. I am doing this *slowly*, I am doing this *incrementally*. Deliberately and subtly. This is attention to detail, this is patience and courtesy. I am using this to do that.

I am explaining how all of these things lead up to this thing.

The hostages thing, the doors-are-locked thing. The imminent foreclosure thing.

This is a narrative progression, ma'am. A throughline, if you will, a discernible plot, so *that's* a little bit about me, so that's good, we're sharing. And what else, what else. [Looks up, thinking.] I stopped masturbating. [Pauses. Silence.] Thank you, I miss it, I do, I miss masturbating. I think about it, you know? I think about picking it back up, and by "it" I mean the act, not my wiener, right? I don't mean that. I mean, I'm not standing up here in front of you good people talking about picking up my wiener, am I? That's gross, it's *gross*, is what it is. Save that kind of talk for the orgy guys, is what I say! But, no seriously, I think the thing I miss most about masturbating, and I've thought about this, I have. Like a lot. People always ask me, they're like, "What do you miss most about masturbating?," and by "people" I mean "nobody," and by "a lot" I mean "no one ever." Like that's never happened, nobody's ever said to me, "What do you miss most about masturbating?" That's not like a phrase anybody's ever said, I don't think, to me. Like I'm not saying it's never happened, ma'am, you know?

Never say nobody's never said what do you miss most about masturbating, you know that old adage?

That old saying?

That old chestnut? That old Brazil nut? You think anybody ever said that, you think anybody ever said, "What do you miss most about masturbating, Louis?" [Quick nod, winks at audience.] You see what I did there, sir? You C.K. what I did? Nobody's ever said that, I don't think. I've never said it, that's for sure, but you know what I *did* say the other day? I said, uh, to my wife who was still my wife then, what I said to my then-wife was I said, "Next time you're making *quinoa* . . . ?"

[Pauses. Laughs quickly.]

That's what I said, I said, "Next time you're making *quinoa* . . . ?" Like that, like a question, voice trailing off and all that. And I stopped myself, you know? Because how was that going to end, you know? That sentence, that request. Seems benign, but it wasn't, and you know what? It's because right then I realized I wasn't an orgy guy.

No *orgy guy* would say that, would he?

To his *wife*?

Next time you're making *quinoa*?

As a set up for a *joke*?

And I'll be honest, I didn't even finish that sentence, not then, so I'm not going to finish this, I don't think, because we've got a lot to get to tonight folks. A lot and a lot.

We're just getting started.

So what should we do? What do I do, what do I say? And that's the thing, nobody ever tells you this, you know?

I feel like I should just keep talking, get it all out, because time is short, it is, and that's the thing. Nobody tells you when to start. [Smiling, pacing.] Where do we start, where do we start? What do we start *with*, and that's really more of the thing, isn't it? What we start *with*, because there's so much stuff. There's jokes and stories and bits, right? Things that I've done and things that I've got to do, right? And got to be an accounting somewhere, doesn't there?

A settling, ma'am?

A reckoning, ma'am?

An arrangement, ma'am? An if-I-put-this-here-then-maybe-this-happens-type thing, ma'am? [Looks out at audience as if hearing something.] What's that?

You want to know a little bit about me? [Smiles, nods, pretends to crack knuckles.] Okay, then.

A little bit about me.

I was born on the Fourth of July. This is true and you could look it up. A firecracker. Lights and celebration. Cookouts and Tom Petty playing on radios. Heat and sun. Coolers full of drinks. Something everybody likes. You get it, you get it. [Pacing, pacing.] Barbecue and ribs and this is setting scenes, this is waving hands, ma'am. [Smiles quickly.] This is adding up, this is fitting things in or it will, anyway. It will start here and call back and this will mean something, it has to. This is a fact, and this is how we will start if we haven't already.

I have never been good at beginning or ending things, so I guess I will start this at the start now that everything is ending or almost over. I do that a lot, talk like this, like I am now. It may be a nervous habit, a tic. An aural crutch. It may be cancer. I should tell you that now, I think, right up front. There's a cancer I may have. [Pauses, stares out. Concerned look on face.] I don't want to alarm you, ma'am. I *may* have it, I *may have* cancer. It's not a hundred percent, it's tough to tell. I'm assuming I do. It would make sense, right? If I had cancer? It'd explain a lot, wouldn't it? Stands to reason, doesn't it, sir? [Stops, grins, looks out.] That's a thing people say, isn't it? "Stands to reason?" Sure they do, sure they do, and this is good, this makes sense, because it was like this. This place, renovating this place? All the stuff, the junk, the asbestos, the bird shit I cleaned out? It's still here. [Taps center of chest with gun.] It's in my lungs, seething, metastasizing, killing me, it is, and this is good. [Stops, laughs.] Not the me-having cancer, that's not good, ma'am. I'm not, we're not saying that, are you?

Ma'am, you're glad that I have *cancer*? [Eyes wide, mouth open, gun hand covering it, shaking head slowly side to side.] No, it's *good* because it makes *sense*. And things *should* make sense, right? So me getting cancer from this place, it makes me more sympathetic, I think, doesn't it? This is narrative progression, I think.

Here is what you're thinking right now.

You're thinking, "He may have been diagnosed with cancer and that with his impending divorce and bankruptcy has forced him to do this, forced him to take hostages, or pretend to take hostages or whatever it is that he is doing. This is sympathy. We can put up with a lot because of this, we the unwilling audience. The building has given him cancer. I feel bad for him and I understand why he's doing what he's doing." This is me doing an impression of you, ma'am, and I'm going to be honest with you, that is *exactly what I want people to think*! I *want* people to feel sympathetic, I do, I declare.

This is sad. [Shakes head, looks down.] I don't have *cancer*, ma'am, at least I don't think I do. It's fake, what I just insinuated was, it's a cheap trick, but all I want is a place in your hearts. It's sad, this whole thing is, but the fact that it isn't true doesn't make it any less sad, does it? Maybe it is true, but it just hasn't happened yet. Maybe I'm getting ahead of myself, maybe I'm jumping the gun. [Holds up gun, hops tiny hop.] I've already said I don't understand time travel, so maybe that helps explain it, but probably not, because I don't know if I remember anymore, I don't, I declare. This place probably killed me.

I went on WebMD the other night. Huge mistake. [Pacing confidently.] WebMD should change its name to "You'reGoingToDieOfCancer.com," shouldn't it? It'sDefinitelyCancer.com? Something like that, right, because there's *nothing you can type in there* that doesn't come back cancer! It's all cancer, ma'am, maybe!

Symptoms, let's see. [Pretends to type.] Uh, scratchy throat? Eyes . . . watery . . . tired . . . and ENTER! [Gives menu face at pretend screen.] Sinuses, allergy, pollen . . . bone cancer? [Looks up, alarmed.] *Bone* cancer? I have *bone cancer*? Because of watery eyes? This seems, that seems odd, right? Odd? Bone cancer? Because I have watery eyes, because I have no appetite? This means cancer? [Looks out, pleading.] But no, I have no appetite anymore, not for anything. Sometimes I think my lack of appetite is somehow tied into the fact that I have no idea what cryptocurrencies are. And I'm not sure why I think this, but I do, kind of. You ever have that, ma'am? A feeling, a hankering? Are these words right? But I don't, I have no appetite for anything I used to have an appetite for, and that includes fried chicken or destruction. If I ever get out of this, I am going to write something beautiful called "We Can Say This Out Loud." A poem or a song, ma'am, either one, either one. If I had a wife, ma'am. If I had a family, ma'am. If they were here to hear. This is what I would do, I think. I'd do it different, maybe. All of this. [Paces, rubs stomach with right hand.] I am smaller now than I was then, then when all this was happening, and this sounds confusing, but it isn't. It's not bad, being smaller isn't. Anyway, we are getting off course here, you and I are, and there's probably a couple of reasons for that. Besides the maybe-cancer, besides the flashing lights, besides the beginning and the end, and what is this, anyway? What is it?

A confession.

I declare, and I'm going to tell you something here, here and now. A confession, a declaration, and it's this, it's this.

I've never really understood time travel. Not in movies, I mean. I don't get it. I am trying to think if I've ever shown a time travel movie here, here in this theater. I don't remember if I have or not. I remember the day I opened this place, opening night. A grand opening. Tuxedos and limousines and passed hors d'oeuvres, ma'am. Pomp, circumstance. I had people handing out socks before they walked in. Socks, ma'am! Can you *imagine*? [Smiling.]

New socks, tube socks, white socks, blue socks. I had people handing out socks to the guests, telling them the socks they had on were about to be blown off. This is what I said, and this was then, this was that night. [Grits teeth, grips gun tight.] I think I am so fucking funny. This is a little bit about me, if we're settling up, if we're declaring. I think this is important to know. Anyway, I took some friends up to the projection booth. The movie was going, the movie was playing. There were platters. Shiny silver discs stacked on a rack. Shiny silver discs racked on a stack, maybe. One or the other. Film was looped through a machine. Gears filling holes on film edges. Fitting perfectly. It was dark, the room was. A movie was showing. Film filming through machine. Wetly coiling, looping in and on itself onto platters. Snaking and disappearing and reappearing. All of this magic. I smiled at my friends in the dark.

I had no idea what was going on.

I understood none of this.

A little bit about me, I am terrible at describing things, but that's it, that's exactly what was happening, right then and there, but that was then, and then was a long time ago, and I've already told you I don't really understand time travel, so I can't be sure about any of this, not really.

[Pauses, squares shoulders, sets feet.]

What this is, is a declaration. And I think we've set that up already, established it. The tone of this thing. It's confessional, it's conversational. Seems to be, anyway. Right now, this is me talking to you, but maybe that will change. It's going to be a long night, folks.

I am going to tell you a lot of things tonight, here, while we have time. These things are going to be true even though it will seem like a lot of them aren't. They will be true even though it will seem like a lot of them shouldn't be. I will talk a lot about sad things, but I will talk a lot about good things, too. I am trying to make this fit, is what I'm doing, all of it. There is so much here, so much to get to. I will work this in any way I can, but you're going to have to bear with me, and what's that, ma'am?

Why?

Why do you have to bear with me? Is that, is that what you said? That's, yeah, that's a good one, that's a good one. Why do you have to bear with me.

Besides the doors being locked?

Besides the bombs?

The trip wires and plastique?

Besides that? Uh, I *guess* because it's polite? It's polite to listen to people? Maybe that's why? And no, and I guess, and I *guess?* I mean, I guess what I'm saying is, now that I'm thinking about it, is that this is kind of shitty. What I'm doing is, anyway. I mean, hostages? Have I come to, has it come to that? It's come to hostages, ma'am? The taking thereof? Heretofore? Let's move beyond that, folks, seriously. Settle down, hunker in. Hunker in? Do people say that? Hunker *down*, I think, not hunker in. *Can* you hunker in? We'll look into that in a second, but first, let's do this. Let's—let me establish some rapport, here. Relate.

So yeah, let's do this, let's get into it, let's rub our hands together [Rubs hands together] and a little bit about *me?*

A little thing I like to *do?*

Like a hobby, you know how people have hobbies? You know how people have things they do? And that's, and I'm laughing now, like this is what I'm going to do, this is how I'm going to start this? I've got like five minutes,

right, and I'm going to spend this first part asking if you
know what hobbies are? This is about right, it's about
right. See what I like to do, ma'am, is I like to hem, and
no, and no, and not hem like sewing, not like that, not
at all. My mother sewed, ma'am, true story. My mother,
the dead one I was just talking about. [Stops. Looks at
crowd blankly.] Was I talking about her earlier? My dead
mother? If not, I should explain. My mother is dead, and
I know I said I was terrible at describing things, but she
is. Dead, I mean.

We good? [Smiles, continues pacing.]

So my mother, she used to sew her own dresses. No
need to, really. She was rich, my dad was too, they were
rich. Rich as Nazis! So much money! So the sewing, my
mother's sewing, it was unnecessary, extraneous, and I say
that *fairly certain* I'm using that word correctly. You ever
do that, ma'am? You ever worry about whether or not
you're using words correctly? Is there a word for that, you
think? Like could it be an answer on a crossword puzzle? The word for worrying about whether or not you're
using words correctly? Maybe it's eleven down? There's a
word for everything, right? A thing in its place, a place
in its thing? You know what they need a word for? You
know what they need a word for, ma'am? [Leaning in,
crouching down, establishing rapport.] They need a word
for that feeling you get when you see like a screenshot
of somebody's phone? And don't, and please. Don't take

this as like some kind of encouragement to bring out your phone. I'm just making a point, here, it's like they're sending you a picture and it's of an image or something that they've got on their phone, and you can see that their battery is low? Like it's like 14 percent or something? And you're like NO! CHARGE YOUR PHONE! Or WHY DO YOU HAVE AT&T? and DO YOU GET APPLE TV PLUS WITH THAT? And you're helpless, right? There's nothing you can do. This isn't *you*, this isn't *your phone*, you know? This isn't even a phone, it's a picture of a phone! It's an image of something from somebody else, it doesn't exist and isn't real and that doesn't *matter*, does it? Because all you see is the red, almost-empty battery, right? And then you check *your* phone, you know? To make sure, to assess, to reassure. [Holds gun up and looks at it like phone, patting it, muttering.] Still green, still green.

No, but there's got to be a word for that, right? Maybe the French have a word for it. They love having words for things and this is what I'm doing, ma'am. Maybe they do, and maybe they don't. Maybe it's a pipe dream, and I am hemming, aren't I? Hemming not like sewing, so let's go back, shall we?

Back to the hemming.

As pertains to the hemming.

In re the hemming.

That is what I do, I hem and I haw. That's a little

bit about me, that's one of my hobbies. I'm into that, into hemming, and into constructing relatable narratives. That's two, maybe three things, depending on how you count. Hemming *and* hawing, ma'am? A activity or two, and I said *ah* again instead of *an*, because I'm fun. Because I'm funny.

Thus the ah.

Ergo the ah.

I had a friend who was going to get into World War II. [Pauses, looks out in audience.] You ever do that, ma'am? You ever have a friend who's about to get into World War II? That's relatable, right? Anyway, he called me up one day, said what war should I be into? I'm getting into one, he said. One or two. This was on the phone, this was back then. I said I was going to name a dog I had once World War II, The Dog. I don't remember what he said after that, but he got into World War II. That was a hobby, that's *his* hobby, ma'am, and I'm clarifying here, lest there be any confusion. Lest there be any, right, confusion. [Pacing.] Because *my* hobby, what *I am into*, and I'd like to think we've kind of established that, that I'm a man of hobbies, a hobbyist, if you will, I think we've established, cleared up that this has nothing to do with confusion. My hobby doesn't. Nope, not at all, and I'm shaking my head, and you can see that, right? Quick and tight and side to side? An assertion, an assertion of a negation? That's right, that's what that nod was, ma'am.

That, and probably a lot more. No, what I am into, my hobby if you will, one of them anyway, is constructing a relatable narrative.

Oh, ma'am!

Oh, and smiling and beaming!

Oh, and looking out triumphantly!

Oh, I'll tell ya, there's nothing I enjoy more, not one thing, than constructing a relatable narrative!

You ever do that?

You ever construct a relatable narrative?

It's seriously, it's the best. That's what I like to do. I like to come home after a hard day of whatever it is that I do around here and just construct, you know? Construct the *fuck* out of a narrative, and I'm sorry, and I apologize for that, ma'am, I do. This isn't, that isn't like me, I'm not, I don't talk like that, I don't. I'm a little worked up, is all. What with all the goings on, I guess, but no, constructing, right, right. I *constructed* this whole place, this whole building. This whole where we are now. I did that, I did this, and now it's all gone. [Quick twitch of the lip, flicker.] Gone or about to be, but that's not the point, I don't think. The point is, I like to construct, you know, really *construct* narratives that are like super-relatable! I love it, I do, I do. Sometimes, and I'm looking off in the distance now. I'm gazing, I'm peering, I'm menu-facing. I am looking at something, looking *for* something, is more like it. This is how I look, and between you and me, you see how *relatable* this is? Am I maybe *doing it right now*? It is, and it's hard, ma'am, it's hard to do this, it's hard to declare all of this, but it's funny, it is. You can relate, right? You see what I'm doing, right? It fits, right? [Squints eyes, tilts head, mouth slightly open.] And you see that face? Ma'am? You see the face I'm making and how my eyes are kind of half slit and my head's tilted just a bit and it looks like I'm reading something at a distance? You see that face, my face? That's what I call a menu face. [Still squinting eyes, tilting head, mouth slightly open.] Let's see . . . You know how invariably, how like every time you look at a menu, like one that's up on a sign, you act like you've never seen one before? What *is* this strange thing, you say? I declare! You study it, you peer. [Makes menu face.] Let's see . . . what is a *Big Mac*? Is there a *Bigger* Mac? You know, Ma'am, how you sometimes make the menu face? That's funny, right? But people make that face all the time, I see it here constantly. Or I saw it here, I guess I should say. People would always ask where the bathrooms were. Like always. It's a pretty small lobby and the lobby has signs and these signs said Bathroom. Or they said Men's Room. Or they said Women's Room, doesn't matter, who cares. Point is, invariably and every single time, when people would come out of the theater, they would ask where the bathrooms were.

They'd do this constantly.

"Where are the bathrooms?" they would say.

"Do you have bathrooms?" they would say.

Do you have bathrooms? [Pausing, looking up. Menu-facing.]

Ma'am, do I have bathrooms? [Smiling.]

Is that a question?

That's something we can ask each other?

That's an appropriate question? When was the last time you went anyplace, and that place didn't have bathrooms? Has it happened in your lifetime? [Shaking head, looking concerned.] It hasn't? Of course it hasn't. [Looks down.]

Again, small space. There's like one or two places these bathrooms could be. This isn't a Rubik's cube. This wasn't that, but inevitably, someone would say, "Where are the bathrooms?"

They would look up.

They would look. Up. At the ceiling. That's not a normal reaction. Do you think that the bathrooms are on the ceiling? They aren't.

This isn't an *Escher print*, sir. They're not *up*. Anyway, there's no call for that kind of talk now, is there? Bathroom humor? We're already at that point? It's funny, though, isn't it? This whole thing? What? No, and where were we, no, sometimes I'm in here doing whatever it is that I'm supposed to be doing and all I can think about is coming home and constructing some really relatable narratives. Maybe that's part of the reason I'm here right now, why we're here, now that I think of it. I've spent so much *time*, ma'am, so much *time* constructing really, super-duper relatable and accessible *narratives* that I lost track of the whole running-a-business, being-a-husband-and-father thing, you know? Like it slipped my mind, like it got lost somewhere, you know? And that's a possibility, isn't it? That it got lost? You've seen what this place looked like before, haven't you? On TV, in the papers? A disaster, right? So full of everything, right? Junk and rubble and shit. Everything, and so much, and you couldn't even see. Insane. So it got lost, right? Whatever it was we were just talking about, it got lost somewhere in the middle of all this narrative constructing. That makes sense, doesn't it? [Nods, smiles, walks across stage.] I declare!

I really enjoy doing it, I do, the narrative constructing, I think because I'm so *good* at it. It could be the only thing I'm really good at, come to think of it. I mean, I'm no good at running a business, obviously. I'm not a good movie theater owner, I'm not. I'm not good at tying ropes. Nooses and whatnot, we established this already? Has this part happened yet? The nooses? And let's not, right? Draw parallels here, right? [Looks out at audience, laughs, shakes head.] No, no those are two things, ma'am, two separate things. [Holds mic hand out to the side.] It's like *here's* my not-being-good-at-business and [Holds hand out on other side] *here's* my not-being-good-at-tying-ropes. These are two separate things, ma'am, which is Okay, right? There can be separate things, right? The only thing in the middle of these two things is me, right? These two facts, these two truths? And I'm confessing, ma'am, I'm declaring. [Quick smile, quick wince. Pauses. Puts arms down, continues walking.] Anyway, I'm no good at explosive making, either, but that? I mean, come on. How would I know how to do something like that? Live and learn, I guess. [Smiles.] You figure it out.

Chapter Two
Here Goes

See, and there, right there, that's honesty, that's something. This is good, this is good to get this all out there.
Put it all out on the table, all of it, I declare. [Looks out,
slowly nods head, slowly.] This is how it is, this is how
I'm going to do this, and it's going well, I think, this
could work. [Smiling, walking.] You know, the pressure's
on with a title like *An Evening of Romantic Lovemaking*.
Because, I mean, that seems like a lot, right?

A lot of lovemaking?

An entire *evening's* worth? That's what you guys came
for, right? You weirdos. Come for the lovemaking, stay
for the hostage-taking. That old adage, ma'am. That old
chestnut. That old Brazil nut. The bar is set *high*, isn't it,
with a title like that? High in the sky, and I don't know
if I'm ever going to be able to live up to this. How *could*
I? What could I *do*, really, to justify this? There's no way

I'm going to be able to live up to this. [Looks out into light.] I'm going to fail, right? Aren't I going to? I have no choice *but* to fail. I've already failed, right? By anybody's definition, and an entire *evening's* worth?

First of all, and let's look at this, an "evening's worth" is a long time, ma'am, to be doing anything, right? And by doing that I've really, I've hamstrung my efforts? Is that it? Ham-stringed them? We could look that up, we could Google it, but I'd appreciate it if you didn't.

No phones, no Googling, for reasons I'm sure you understand. Cop reasons, ma'am.

Hostage reasons, ma'am.

Impending doom reasons, ma'am, but don't sweat it, and don't worry, I have a bit later on about Google, honest, I do. This will tie in and I guess now I bracket something? Ma'am? [Looking into light, pleading look on face.] My point is that an evening of any kind of anything is a long time, right? But an evening of *romantic lovemaking*? Romantic, ma'am! A specific *type* of lovemaking!

Heretofore!

Forthwith!

And here comes the defendant and *romantic lovemaking*? I mean, and I'll say it, I'm not into making love. No, I'm not, it's not, I'm just not interested in it. Not really, and not like it's not like I'm, whatever, you know? I mean, it's fine, that's fine, lovemaking is, and there was a time where I was really interested in it. How interested, ma'am? Was that you who said that? Great question! A great and sexy question that I'm not going to answer, as I don't see how it pertains, ma'am. Is germane, ma'am, but trust me, trust me, I declare. Anyway, no, but I was interested in lovemaking, I guess. I thought I actually might be an orgy guy, but not anymore. Not really, but I don't know, so anyway this is going to be a long evening, ma'am, an evening's worth of me getting nowhere. Like, I don't see how we're ever getting out of here [Laughs], I *don't*.

Like any of us, I can't see us walking out of here. Because it's taken years to get *here*, so if you think you're going to get out in an hour? [Laughs, shakes head.] I mean, no, oh no. And I'm laughing because it's funny and I'm shaking my head because I just said I was and you might want to call *home*, you know? Check on the children. Make sure they're Okay, but no, we can't call, right? Nobody can call anybody, nobody can say anything, isn't that right? [Looks out, menu-faces crowd.] Isn't that how this is, how nobody can say anything or something? So much something so close to another thing or something? Maybe it is, and maybe it doesn't matter. I used to read sad stories a lot, too. Sad stories and sometimes detective stories. I'd love to write a sad detective story sometime, but doubt I'll get the chance. We're going to be here for a while, is what I'm saying, get comfortable.

Sure, I'm laughing and smiling, but sometimes it

hurts, and I'll just put this out there, it hurts because of these sores I have in my mouth. [Sips bottle of water, pretends to spit.] And it could be cancer. And it's a confession, right? A declaration? That's what this is? So this is fine, me saying this. Like, I'm getting these *sores*, and can I just talk about this for one second? [Sips, pretends to offer it to crowd.] I have these *sores* in my mouth, and I'm kind of whispering now, because they *hurt*. I have them now, but they're going away, but I have them.

Sores, ma'am.

Mouth, ma'am.

My, ma'am.

You ever have sores in your mouth, sir? You know how you sometimes get *sores* in your mouth, like *canker sores?* You know the word *riddled?* Have you heard people say the word *riddled*, ma'am? You know how sometimes people say the word *riddled*, how that's a word people say? That's what I am, ma'am, I'm riddled with sores. Oh my gosh. They hurt so bad, I can't talk, which is bad because all I *do* is talk, or think about talking, or talk about thinking, whatever. I have sores in my mouth that prevent me from talking about thinking. You ever have that? You ever think, where's the stage direction gone? So I'm like I've got to do something with these sores. I've got to talk my way out of these sores, you know? Because, and let me clarify, ma'am, because I can't tell if I've made these things happen by talking about them. Maybe I've done something? I've caused this, I've caused these, these sores? This is in response to that, to this? [Waves arms up and around.] To all of this? A relation, ma'am, a correlation? There's a correlation between this, all of this, and my sores? That's what this is, that's the sore-sitch? [Looks out, confused, menu-facing.] And what's this, and that's what this is? A declaration? It's a mess, ma'am, it's a mess, and a whole evening of *this*? [Looking around, squinting into light.] What's romantic about *this*, ma'am? Sores? Is this part of my cancer? Should I WebMD, should I Google? Do a little sore-Googling, a pre-romantic lovemaking sore-Google? That's no good, and that, what that was, what all of that was has nothing to do with what we are here for tonight, which is an evening, ma'am. An evening of romantic lovemaking.

[Stops, pauses. Stares out, confused.]

Should we do something else? How much time do I have? I feel like I'm losing you, folks, not like you're going anywhere, but you know what I mean. I feel like I lost you there for a little bit, which doesn't seem fair, really. I mean, since when does all of this have to entertain? I can't digress, I can't diverge? I can't talk about sores? This is all about you? This can't be a little bit about me?

Here's a little bit about me, folks, here's something you can probably relate to, I get scared sometimes. About things, people, situations. I do. It's true, I know, sounds illogical. Sounds improbable, ma'am, I know it, I do, but

it is. And I know what you're thinking. You're thinking,
"You? You up there? With the gun? Striding so confidently? So self-assuredly? You, who figured out how to
renovate this building? You, who figured out how to rig
up these doors with explosives? You, who says 'rigger'
without even a tinge of self-consciousness?"

Yep. Me.

I do, ma'am, I do. [Smiling earnestly, smiling sin-
cerely.] We all do. We're all scared, we all get nervous.
When I get nervous? [Looks around from side to side
then leans in.] When I get nervous, my upper lip
twitches. Tinily, almost imperceptibly, ma'am. It does. A
little twitch, a little tell. You probably couldn't see it, but
I feel it. It's this tug, ma'am, and it's like my nostril kind
of flares and it kind of pulls on my upper lip, just a little.
That's my tell, ma'am, and I know it's not much, but it's
there. [Stops, thinks.] You ever see that movie about the,
I think, poker players? There's these guys, these kids, and
they like play poker, high-stakes poker? And they like
have to play this big Russian mob guy or something,
who is like really good at cards, like the best at cards?
[Looks out at crowd. Menu-faces.] You ever see this? And
nobody can beat this guy, this Russian, and he's always
beating everybody at cards. There's all these shots of him
sitting at the poker table, eating Oreos, beating the shit
out of everybody at cards, have you seen this? Anyway,
and I don't remember a lot of it, except that it turns out

that *this guy* has a tell, the Russian guy does. It turns out
[Leans in, looks quickly, eyes wide, side to side, then out
at crowd] *eating Oreos* is this guy's tell. Like every time he
was going to bluff or call or whatever, he'd eat an Oreo.
That was his deal. Eating cookies. Pretty stupid, isn't it?
But that was like the whole twist of that movie, the fact
that eating Oreos was that guy's tell. Sounds like a long
way to go, doesn't it?

One time I said to my then-wife, "I bet I can make
that lady tug at her sweater." We were in the store and this
kind of overweight lady was walking toward us, and by
kind of overweight I mean fat. She was fat, and no, and
groan, and relax. [Looks out disapprovingly at crowd.]
Grow up, folks. I mean, if not now, when? This is life, this
is reality, I declare, and time is running out. So anyway,
I knew that if I *looked* at her, right, if I *gazed* at her, then
she would feel uncomfortable.

How did I know that, ma'am? [Looks out, smiles.]

How did I know that she'd do that?

How did I know that she'd tug on her sweater, just
a little bit. How did I know that she'd try to adjust, to
rearrange? To straighten, to smooth out? To cover and
hide? How did I know that? Is that what you're asking
me? I just did. [Nods at another point in crowd.] Ask
this guy, he gets it.

Anyway, that's a shitty thing to do, ma'am, it's terrible,
I know. But I said to my then-wife, I said watch this. She

was a fat lady, and groan, and I know, and don't. [Raises eyebrows, quick nod at gun, quick shake of head.] I'm sorry, but some people are fat. They are. That's not, we can't, you know. I'm not gonna stand up here and say otherwise, right? In this declaration, in this reckoning? I'm supposed to eschew, here? I'm supposed to obfuscate? I'm supposed to say something isn't something? We're not past all that, all of us aren't? We're about to die, people, everybody here's about to die. Do you understand that? I mean, I don't know much more clear? Clearer? Clearly? I don't how much clearer I can make this, like I don't know how. This is real, this is happening, and I don't know what we don't understand about this. Fat people are fat. Things can be things, ma'am. How is this confusing? How is any of this confusing? You see this, right? [Holds up gun.] This gun? Do I need to eat an Oreo? Do I need to tug on my fat shirt? We're *all going to die.* [Waves gun around side to side.] Everybody in this room, no question about that, right? You didn't come in here thinking you were going to leave alive, right? [Stops, laughs.] Well, I mean, you probably *did*, right? I mean, you *probably* did, right, why wouldn't you? You came in here to see a movie or something, to see *An Evening of Romantic Lovemaking* or whatever. You didn't expect to be held hostage, I'm assuming, but I'm talking in *general*, ma'am!

I'm talking long term!

I'm talking big picture, right, you know how this ends!

It ends with every single one of us dying. And it's always ended like that, it's never not ended like that. [Laughs, paces.] In every version of this story, it always ends up like that.

Anyway, what were we talking about?

Lips?

Quivering lips?

My lips?

I'm standing up here talking about my lips? Lips don't lie, ma'am, somebody sang that, or something goddamn close to it. [Laughs.] No, but what are we talking about? I don't have any idea, I don't. I'm just throwing shit out there, you know? Everything that's happened and everything that's going to happen, I guess, I'm not sure. This all goes in, all of it does, and the only way to do it is just do it, I guess, so here goes.

Chapter Three

I Miss Masturbating

So we should start, I guess, even though we've started before. Before and again, ma'am, before and again and a little bit about me, I don't really understand time travel? Like, I don't get it. I may have said this before, but it's true. I don't and I do not, no, not like the actual how-to-do-it, because no one knows how to do it, but like movies? You ever see a time travel movie? You know what I mean, and like, I don't understand. I mean, I get part of it, like you go back in time, I get that. I get that you travel. But then it's like you can't *do* anything because then you're the guy from before that you used to be before you turned into the, you know what I mean? And then I'm just like, I can't fucking do this, you know? You know what I mean? There always comes a point where I'm like, "I don't know what the fuck this is," you know? You ever do that? You ever watch a movie or read a book or see something on TV and start watching it and all of a sudden you're like, "I don't know what the fuck anyone's saying anymore." You know? Like, what?

Who is this guy?

What is he supposed to do?

Was he here the whole time? And maybe that's just me, and maybe that's just me, and maybe everybody else just *gets* everything. You ever get the sense that everybody else just *gets* everything? And you don't get *anything*? Like I get that, I get the sense that I don't get anything. Like right now.

I *kind* of know what's happening, sort of, and here's how this is going in my head, and it's pretty straightforward.

I'm here.

You're there.

Doors are locked.

There's some sort of *bomb*? That's been *rigged*?

In this set of circumstances, I'd be considered a *rigger*? Can you say *rigger*? In this climate? The age we are in?

Can I say that?

Did I?

Is this bad, he asked, stridently? This is uncomfortable, ma'am, I get that, I do. It's uncomfortable, the saying of things and all that. It's a quivering lip, a concealing tug. The saying of things that *sound* like things, that's uncomfortable, it is, and nobody likes it . . . I get that.

And these are just words, just words, and this is to say nothing about locks on doors.

This is to say nothing of guns and threats, of films in cans, of cancers, of divorce. Of lovemaking, romantic or otherwise.

And it's uncomfortable and hard to understand, and that's not what I'm trying to do here, not even a little bit, because here's what this is.

A declaration, right?

Simple and straightforward.

To the point.

Nothing convoluted, nothing cryptic.

Guy buys old movie theater.

Guy renovates it.

Acclaim, prestige.

Things go good.

Things go not good.

Guy goes bankrupt.

Drinking, anger, depression.

A wife and a child.

A thing and then another thing.

Guy loses building, wife, kids, name.

Failure and shame. A sick, sinking feeling. Maybe cancer.

Guy gets desperate, guy takes hostages, guy blows everything up, fade to black, end scene, credits roll. I mean, we *get that*, right?

The progression, the narrative whatever-the-fuck?

Easy to follow, right?

Not like *time travel*, which as I've pointed out, I have no idea what the fuck *that* is, right?

Seriously ma'am, [Leaning in, hunkering] you expecting me to understand time travel? With all its complexities and nuances? This seems like a *lot*, doesn't it? Even for you, who I can *barely see*, but who I'm *pretty sure* exists right? Here's one thing that I *do* think about time travel. You know how in *time travel* movies, when people realize that they're back in time and they're like *don't fuck anything up*, you know what I mean? They're like *don't do anything*, don't *touch anything*, because if you *do* something, then it's like, you know, then something else will happen. A reaction to that action. [Small smile.] I know, I'm great at describing things, but no, you do something, anything, and then you become your dad, or a butterfly, or Hitler, or whatever. So you shouldn't *do* anything, because it's like everything you do, even if you were to go back two weeks in time.

A scant two weeks, ma'am.

A fortnight, ma'am, if you will.

One fortnight!

Ah fortnight!

My kids play Fortnite. I have no idea what they're talking about or what they're doing. I sit there and I watch these beautiful kids of mine, my beautiful boys, shoot people in the face and ambush people and build stupid forts and do stupid dances, and I love them so much. I was watching them just the other day, before they left. [Pauses, stops, confused. Blinks hard, continues.]

But no, if you did *that* and you started fucking around with stuff, you started moving anything, or anything you did, anything you did would be *fraught* with repercussions, right? Like you have *no idea* what would happen. It could be *monstrously bad*, right? But everything you do is dripping with significance, everything that you would do in that situation. We all agree on this, right? We're not disagreeing?

I'm not. [Points into crowd.]

That guy isn't.

And I'm declaring this to you. Like I'm *declaring* this to you. I aver and avow. *But*, and this is a huge but, backing up right here folks, I'm warning you. *But*, the present is always about ready to become the past. Like this just now is the past and so is this, and this, and you get it, you see, snake eating its tail and all that nonsense, and if that's the *case*, and it is, then why don't we feel the same sense of urgency about everything we're doing *now*, you know what I mean? Like why isn't *now* fraught with significance? Why aren't people going, "Shit, should I *do* that, because in the future that could fuck everything up."

We have zero sense of this!

It's, do whatever the fuck you want!

Go fucking nuts, go buy a theater! You know what you're doing, right? How fucking hard can this *be?* Ignore your wife and family, get so far up your own fucking ass, you don't know what's what, right? You know, no repercussions, right, that's what I'm saying, and this is probably a great theory somewhere, but again, I'm not a smart person. And this is something a smart person would think. I've always been envious of smart people. I'm friends with smart people. I'd like to be smart—sometimes I think I *could* be smart. You ever do that, you ever be like, "I'm going to be smarter?" Like a, like a New Year's Resolution? I'm not sure I'm going to have one this year, probably because I'll be dead. [Crouches down.] Ma'am, how do you think my being dead will impact my ability to carry out my New Year's Resolution? Will it hinder it, me being dead? Like I'm probably not going to be learning Spanish while dead? *Muy muerto,* ma'am? *No learno Español?* No, *no es bueno.* Spending time with the kids, will that, can I do that, you think? Being a dead guy and all?

I have kids. Had kids? I'm still here, right? [Looks down, taps head with mic.] Boys, ma'am, I have boys. I don't have any girls, and I'm *glad* that I don't have any girls because from what I understand, it's not easy being a woman and all. I'll be honest with you ladies: it looks *terrible!* [Laughs.] Everything about it seems *unbelievably* bad.

Periods, you know?

Rape?

[Looks out, shocked. Shakes head.]

No, I'm *saying!* It's *bad*, I'm not, I'm not trivializing. These are bad, rape is bad. I said it. I said it, folks, I did. I took a stand. I put it out there, I declare and a lot of people would've come in here tonight? Maybe they have good things to say about rape? Maybe they do. Not me. I don't have *anything* good to say about it. At all.

I mean, I guess I *could* say something about how with date rape, at least the woman gets a date. I could say something like, 'Maybe we should concentrate more on the date part and less on the, you know . . .' [Eyebrow raise, quick tilt of head.] I could say I'm a glass half full of rape guy, but I'm not. That's not *relatable*, ma'am. That's not endearing me as a narrator, and where am I going with this? Where am I going with this?

You know who's different, is ah, men and women. I find that that's true. Like my then-wife, I don't have any idea what she's talking about half the time. She doesn't *care* what I'm talking about, and that's fine. "You think you're so goddamn funny," she said to me more than once. Said it the other day, actually. It was the day I was going to go have a colonoscopy, and should we do that now, make colonoscopy jokes? [Smiles, scratches head with gun hand.] A bloody-stool joke, just to soften things up? Will *this* help move the narrative, will it endear me to you? Let's set the stage a bit. [Stands up straight, deep breath, brushes imaginary dust off shoulders.]

I'm going to get a colonoscopy. It was my New Year's Resolution. No, actually, the *reason* I'm getting a colonoscopy is because the *other day* when I was going to the bathroom, there was blood everywhere, and let me say that again, ma'am, let me emphasize. Imagine if you will, he said theatrically. [Squatting down.] I'm on the toilet, and where are the bathrooms in the place anyway? Anyway, I wiped and saw blood everywhere! All over the toilet paper, ma'am! A bloody mess!

I know!

Blood!

Terrifying!

And the bowl is full of blood, ma'am. [Laughing, surprised.] A terrible scene!

Oh my, I said, and I said this out loud. I said oh my looking at all the blood. I thought about WebMDing it, you know, but didn't, because you know how that story ends, right? I've done that part already? So I call an actual doctor, my actual doctor, and I'm on the phone with some lady. Sheena.

The receptionist. She asked why I was calling. What is the purpose of your call? she said. I said I wanted to have a colonoscopy, I guessed. [Crouches down, smiles.] I made a joke with her because that is what I *do*, ma'am. I made a joke with Sheena.

I said, "It's not like I *want* to get one."

"It's not like it's my life-long dream or anything."

I said, "It's not like I'm *dying* to get this done, don't get me wrong." We both laughed at that. I am very funny, ma'am, in here and in real life. So anyway, Sheena. She asked for my birth date. She wanted to see if I was in the system, she said, so I told her. I wondered if I was in the system, if I *could* be in the system and not even know it, about what that would mean.

So I told her.

I said this is a little bit about me, Sheena. This was on the phone, this was after the blood, I declare.

I said I was born on the fourth of July, like America, like my Uncle Kenny. I said this, said this just like that, except the part about my Uncle Kenny, because there was no reason to. She knew it was America's birthday though. Everybody knows that, so we didn't mention that. Sometimes when I tell people my birthday, they say stuff about firecrackers.

All those firecrackers just for you, they say.

You're a real firecracker, they say.

You are hemming, you are hawing, they say.

You are digressing.

Then Sheena asked me my name and I didn't say anything. Not a word, ma'am. I was staring at the phone, the phone in my hand. She asked for my name and I didn't say anything. I had no idea, ma'am. [Looking out, eyes wide.] I was stumped. I just sat there. Sat there where I was, sitting at a desk or standing, pants and underpants and shirt. There I was, not knowing if I was racist or alive or dead, not knowing my own name, just like that, just like that.

Sheena said hello and then she said hello again. I had no idea, because I had no idea what was going on, not one, and what were we talking about? Not colonoscopies, I know that much. Let me think, let me think. [Taps head with gun, sucks air through teeth. Smiles, remembering.]

Oh yeah, yeah! Men and women! Different! They are so different, am I right?

Ladies, Harvey Weinstein, huh?

Yeah.

Hollywood producer was doing gross things. That's a shocker! Weren't we *shocked*?

We were like, "what?" you know?

One guy was like, "Huh?"

Some guy was like, "Dag!" you know? You know how sometimes people are all like "dag!" when they hear something? You know how that is, ma'am, he asked, desperately trying to make a connection? [Crouches down, eyes wide, peering out and out.] And this is probably part of it, maybe, I don't know. Part of the declaring? I declare? [Standing back up, pacing.] Well this guy was like that, ma'am, he was all like, "Dag!" when he heard about this guy masturbating in front of women. He was all like *et tu*, Harvey? And then after this Weinstein fella, there were like all these other men, all these other Hollywood type men, and it turns out that *they* were masturbating in front of women, too!

What? Everybody is masturbating in front of women?

And that was me, that was what I was like when I heard about all these guys masturbating in front of women. And here's my take on that, folks, because nobody was asking. My take on that whole thing was like, is this something that people are doing? They're masturbating in front of women? Like just walking around masturbating in front of women? This is something people do? I got to be honest, it never occurred to me, not once. I'm forty-six years old, that's damn near fifty, and it never, not once crossed my mind to masturbate in front of a woman. I'm not sure how I should feel about that. Conflicted? I guess, I mean, I guess, but that's not, we're not, what are we talking about again? Women? And men? Masturbating? Why would you want to masturbate in front of people? I haven't masturbated in years, that's true, it is. I miss it, though, I do.

The masturbating.

I think what I miss the most about masturbating is probably the orgasms. [Serious look.] Like of all the things I miss about masturbating, that's probably, [Smiles] that's probably thing one I miss. No seriously, I miss the orgasms that I would have as a direct result.

Of the masturbating I was doing, which was a lot, if we're being honest, and if we can't be honest now, ma'am? Here, ma'am? With the sirens about to come and the flashing lights and the tear gas, I'm assuming? We can be honest, is what I'm saying. I can tell you these things, share these things. That's nice, it is.

But no, masturbating, that was fun. [Laughs.] But I don't do it anymore because it's not good, you know? I mean, it just isn't, and I could get into a whole thing about self-*control*, and God, and *morality* and the degradation of the *soul*, and all that, I could, but you would all think I was some kind of nut, right? A nut-job? A Brazil nut, mayhap? Perchance? And the *last* thing I would want for you folks to think is that, because when you get out of here? And you will get out of here, it's only an evening, right? Of romantic lovemaking? When you get out of here, I want you to think kindly on what happened here tonight. This was hard for me, it was. To do all this. To bare and share. Baring and sharing is caring, is what they say, right? They say this even when they don't. They may have already said it for all we know, right? Could be saying it right now. But let's finish this part right now. Women and men, right? Women and men?

Women and men.

But women, it's tough, right? It's tough. And I say that in all sincerity, it's very *hard*. And I can't imagine what it would be like to be a woman and to be *objectified*, you know? To be from almost, you know, cradle to grave, just this consistent objectification, and being *belittled* and *demeaned* and diminished and ignored and when you're *not* ignored, you're being *sexualized* and marginalized and, you know, *raped!*

Groped!

People are *beating off* in front of you! It's terrible and you have to walk around and you're *afraid*, you know? And think about that for a second, sir, think about having to walk around your entire life being afraid. Think how horrible that would be, how that would warp and taint *every single interaction* you had, this fear would? Are you imagining this? *Can* you imagine this? A life riddled by fear? Consumed and subsumed? This constant, ever-present fear? Looming and lingering and impending? And this is it, sir, this their reality, women's reality, and it's awful, it is, it is. They live in *fear*, and are *objectified*, *sexualized*, *trivialized*, belittled, demeaned and ignored, right? Terrible!

But they get to wear *boots*.

[Smiles.]

They get to wear boots, like big boots, you know what I mean? Big, thigh-high boots! Like whenever they want, they can *do* that!

I can't do that! [Pacing.] Like if I walked into the grocery store with a pair of thigh-high boots? And a huge *scarf* wrapped around my neck? I couldn't do that. Not a chance.

People would comment, ma'am!

Eyebrows raised, ma'am!

Askew and askance, ma'am! They'd say things like "What's the deal with those boots? And that huge scarf?" they'd say, things like that. And ma'am, that's another impression right there. That's my impression of what people might say if I showed up wearing thigh-high boots and a huge scarf. How'd I do? Did I nail it? I feel like I nailed it, but what? Scarves? Listen to how I say that.

Scarves.

Scarves.

Ridiculous, right? I declare! What's the deal with these *scarves*, all of a sudden? Like I go out, I see women wearing these *huge fucking scarves* all over the place? Is this what we're doing now? We're all just going to wear huge fucking scarves, ladies? Is that right? I'm trying to figure this out. Women wear huge fucking scarves and men are walking around masturbating? Is there a correlation here? A scarf-masturbation correlation? Maybe women could *use* these scarves to clean up after these men ejaculate all over the place. And I know, and I know. Groan and grimace, groan and grimace, and hold on, this makes sense. I am on to something here, I think, but let's, ma'am? [Peers out into crowd.] Don't let me forget this part, this is good, this is good, but we're on a tight schedule here and I'm not sure how this is going to fit in.

Masturbating scarves?

Boots?

The fuck is going *on here?*

This is a relatable narrative?

This is romantic lovemaking?

You call *this* a hostage situation? This *doesn't fit*, ma'am, this is *sub-par*, ma'am, sub-par at best! But back to my original point, on the one hand there's the fear of being raped and on the other hand, you know, boots. Boots and scarves. I'm not saying it's a *good* trade-off, I'm not saying it's *even*. [Holds hands out on either side, balancing like a scale.] But I'm a half-full kind of guy. I'm a lemons and lemonade guy. I mean, no, nobody's beating off in front of me and I don't worry about getting raped, but I also couldn't wear capri pants, which is something I think I'd like to do.

You know what I mean when I say capri pants, ma'am? Sir? capri pants? You know, we know? We're understanding each other, this is a relatable narrative? A discernible throughline? This season, all the best throughlines are discernible, I'm told.

Those capri pants, they're lazy right? I see those capri pants, I joke about them. Ma'am, I'm going to make jokes about capri pants, you know what I mean? I'm only human. I'm a human being ma'am, a hack like everybody else. I'm going to go to the capri pants well, I'm going to go after the low-hanging pants fruit. I'm not proud. Can you say *pants fruit?* But anyway, pants, right? capri pants, they go all the way to the end, but not quite, you know? They go to like mid-calf and then just stop.

Finished.

Finito.

Pantsnito.

They drive me crazy, they do, they do. Finish, I scream at them! Finish! What a lazy pant. Seriously, ma'am? Sir? Is there a lazier pant? I declare.

The capri pant is like, "You know what? Fuck it. We're done." There was a show called *Party of Five*, and this was like maybe twenty years ago. I never saw it, the show I mean. I don't know anything about it, which is a lie, because I obviously do, right? That would be a fucking stupid way to start a story, wouldn't it be? Like you go up and you're like, "I have no idea what I'm talking about, but hear me out."

Not ideal, not ideal. But, and again, this is a huge but, backing up right now, but it's not like you're going anywhere, right? You put the captive back in captive audience. And seriously, you know how sometimes you're like, "I'd rather kill myself than listen to this for five more fucking seconds?" You know how you've said that?

Ma'am, you've said it.

Sir? You know you have. That guy over there's *thinking* it, but he's not, no, he's not saying anything, is he.

That fucking guy right there. [Smiles, shakes head knowingly.] He's a smart one.

He's like, "Let's play this out."

He's like, "I bet he's bluffing."

He's like, "This motherfucker knows how to rig an explosive? *This* motherfucker does? The same mother-fucker who was googling 'how to tie a noose?'"

Anyway, no, you guys, you guys can test that right now. Go ahead. If this is too much, too whatever, too I-gotta-get-the-fuck-out-of-here, fine, just head for the doors. Hit the exits, see what happens if you don't want to hear me talk about capri pants, and boots, and scarves, and the inequalities. There's the door. Me with the may-be-cancer, me with the abandonment, with the bank-ruptcy and foreclosure. You just go ahead. Leave like everybody leaves. Tell my kids I said Hi, I'll wait.

I'll wait. [Folds arms across chest. Taps foot.]

We're back now? We're good? We're all listening?

Ok, where were we?

Party of Five, yeah, I've never seen it, [Continues walking, pacing] but from what I gather it's about five people who are having a party. Jennifer Love Hewitt was in it, right, and she wore *sweaters*, and they were kind of *long* sweaters, like the sleeves, and she would kind of put her hands so that the sweater would kind of cover most of her hands, you know?

Am I doing a good job of describing this, folks?

Am I painting a good sweater picture?

And that was kind of her thing on *Party of Five*, she

kind of *did* that, you know? Am I making this up? Did any of this happen? I'm saying this like it's a fact, but I don't know if it's true. I think it is. It is. And that was kind of her thing, like her sleeves would cover most of her hands and her fingers would be kind of poking out, and there's a correlation there, right? Between the sleeves and the pants? You see where I'm going with this, why I thought of this right now? And I am assuming this makes sense, that it should go on the list, right? Anyway she did this, Jennifer Love Hewitt did this, and then everybody started doing it. Like having their fingers poke out of their sweater or whatever I'm talking about. Everybody did that.

Oh, we just *do* that, we said. We just all wear our sweaters like that!

No, you don't! You don't wear your sweaters like that! That's, what is that called, ma'am? That thing where you do something you're not supposed to because you're not the thing, or whatever?

Appropriation! That's what this is, what that is, that's appropriation! People talk about Moana, you know how people say you can't dress up like Moana? The Disney Moana? You can't dress up like her because you're not Moanan, or whatever? Stop doing that, is what I say. If they wanna dress up like Moana? If that's what they Moana do, and oh my God, ma'am? Sir? What I just did there? If that's what they *Moana* do? Fuck, I've wasted my life, haven't I, and what? No, no, if that's what they

Moana do, then let them! Not a big deal! Stop making a big deal about everything, and this is what's interesting to me, is that everything is simultaneously the biggest deal that's ever happened and also totally pointless, right? So which is it? So if everything's *in*-consequential and it *doesn't* matter, and blah blah blah, whatever, and there's not a point, there's not a connection? Then is everything *pointless* or does it have nothing *but* point, and it's one or the other, here. It's not both. My friend who looks Jewish but isn't said that new pencils were pointless and this is a joke I have either told already or will sometime later on, tough to say, tough to say. Anyway, it's out there now, which is good, and that's half of it right there, right?

Chapter Four
Nobody Knows What a Cat Is

But anyway, and we were what now? Talking about masturbating? About masturbating *in front of people*? And I'll be honest with you, it never occurred to me to do that, it takes a different breed of cat, I guess, a different breed of cat. I have a theory about cats. Cats are like men and women are like dogs, right? Something like that, isn't that a book? I don't think anybody knows what a cat is.

Hear me out.

A little bit about me: my dog just died, right? [Shocked look. Eyes wide, aghast.] I know, I know.

Insult and injury, ma'am!

Piling on, ma'am!

And at this point, it just sounds like I'm making shit up, doesn't it? Failed marriage, bankruptcy, shame, ruin? Embroiled in the middle of a fucking *hostage* situation? Taking *hostages?*

Check, check, check, and check and now *dead dog?*

Dead fucking *dog*, ma'am?

Are we stretching it here, ma'am?

The limits of credulity, ma'am?

Enough, already!

But it's true, my dog died, and no, and yeah, it was really sad, I was very upset. I loved that dog, I did, I did. Loved her. And I know everybody says their dog is the greatest, and maybe it is, I don't give a shit you know? I mean, I don't, it's your dog, of course you feel that way, I don't care. I don't give a shit about your dog just like you don't give a shit about mine, I know, you know, but *my* dog, she was the greatest, and she died, right? She died, and it was so terrible and in the middle of all this, you know?

Foreclosure, right?

Divorce!

My kids are gone, ma'am, my babies!

My wife has taken them!

Nowhere to be found!

This is not funny!

Why are you laughing?

This is shame and ruin!

This is what this is, this is where we are, and your fucking *dog dies?* This is piling on, right? Isn't it? Ma'am? This is morbidly obese! You know how people say *morbidly* obese? Why morbidly? I wonder. Obese isn't good enough? Like if I say, that guy's obese, we don't get it? We're not, you and I aren't, we're not connecting? There's a gap, a lack? A fat gap, a fat lack? We don't *understand?* But then when I add a *morbidly* to it, all of sudden we're right there, [Points two fingers toward eyes then back out toward audience] we get it, we know what we're saying? Because it's mean, and what are we doing here, what am I saying? Something about a dog? This is relevant? I need to declare this?

One time I read this book about pebbles and a bucket. [Stops, looks out, wide eyed. Smiles.] That's not, no, I mean it wasn't about that, not like the whole book wasn't. That'd be a hell of a book, wouldn't it?

"What're ya reading, there?"

"Oh, you know, just a book."

"Oh yeah? What about?"

"Pebbles and a bucket."

"Huh. Well . . . enjoy."

And . . . scene!

[Clasps hands, quick bow.] That was a scene from my play, ma'am, a play I'm just now writing. I'm not really sure what it's about yet, maybe something about *pebbles and a bucket*, [Looks out, menu-faces] but what were we talking about? Oh yeah, no, you can put a pebble in a bucket, and it's no big deal. You can heft it around, tote it around, right? Swing it around, look at me! But you add enough pebbles in the bucket, you can't lift it anymore, right? Too heavy, right? What with all the pebbles and all, right? The accumulation thereof, sir. It's straws and camel backs, right? You see where I'm going with this, sir. The burden, I can tell you do. The moment you walked in. I said to myself, *here's* a guy who gets it. Said it right out loud, I did, unless I didn't. And it's either one or the other, sir, I did or I didn't, right? That's not, we're not debating that, right? Another thing we're not debating is my dog, my dead dog. Let's focus here, people. Please try and pay attention. Time is short, I've got a lot to declare, I declare, but I loved that dog. Wife did, too. My kids loved her, but she was sick, and she was old, and she couldn't breathe any more. Tumors on her lungs, ma'am. [Smiles. Shakes head.] Fucking tumors. Couldn't sit down, couldn't lie down, because she couldn't breathe when she did, and my heart is breaking now, ma'am. Breaking over a stupid fucking dog and I'm sorry, I'm sorry, this is no way to start this, or be in the middle of this, and I know it, I do. Crying about a dead dog? [Leans forward, conspiratorial look on face.] And I'm really not crying about the dog, am I ma'am? A dog? This is hemming and hawing, isn't it ma'am? This is bush-beating-around, evading and avoiding? I've lost my family, my wife took my children and left, I have lost my business, I'm a disgrace and a failure and a waste. I've taken a room full of people hostage, I'm waving a gun around; there are bombs and explosives and tripwires? Fucking *plastique*, and this is what I'm crying about? About a *dog*?

Did you hear the way I said that?

The disdain?

I'll say it again, about a *dog?* Not likely, ma'am, not likely, but my dog really did die and even though that may not be the only reason I'm getting choked up, it's still pretty sad. She was old, like 14, which is [Stops, pretends to count] that's like who-gives-a-shit in dog years. Is my math right on that, sir? Does that sound good?

[Cups hand to ear, tilts head, looks out.]

What's that?

What kind of dog was she?

Oh, she was like a mutt, like a German Shepherd mutt. Maybe part Rottweiler, I'm not sure. And when I say that, you know what I mean, right? You have an image, you know what I'm saying. There's a commonality. We know what a German Shepherd is, everyone does. We're in this together, we're not alone. You get it, ma'am, right? A German Shepherd? Of course you do, you see it, we all do, and even if doesn't look *exactly* like my dead dog, we're all in the same ballpark, the same dog park. We're all together and we understand. So let's say I said an Irish Setter, like let's say I said my dog died and she was an Irish Setter, you'd know what I was saying.

You'd say, oh yeah, Irish Setter. Like the soap.

And I'd be like no, that's Irish Spring.

And you'd say, oh right, right. Irish Setter, they're magically delicious, and I'd be like no, that's Lucky Charms, I think. The cereal with the leprechaun and then I'd be like no, no, an I-rish Set-ter, like that, like really enunciate, and you'd be like oh yeah, the one with the hair, right? But you'd get it, though, right, but that doesn't work with cats. It doesn't work, I've tried. Nobody knows what a cat is. If I was like, oh my cat died and you said what kind of cat was it, and I said a calico, you'd be like, I don't know what the fuck that is, you know? Nobody knows what a fucking calico is.

I stand up here, I go, "My cat died, she was a tabby."
[Stares blankly.]
Blank fucking stares.
"Yeah, I'm pretty broken up. My calico cat just died."
Nothing.

What the fuck is *that?* What the fuck does that *do?* What are we accomplishing, ma'am, me throwing a dead cat around? Does that make me more sympathetic? Are you more invested in this, [Waves gun around] this evening? No, you aren't, you're more *confused,* if anything. You're going, "Yeah, I was kind of with him, what with all the shit thrown at him and all. The maybe-cancer, the divorce and bankruptcy, the losing everything. I was right *with him,* you know, and then all of a sudden he's up there like 'Boo-hoo, my cat!' and I'm like 'Fuck this guy.'"

Is that right, ma'am? That's right, isn't it, there's nothing tying us together anymore, nothing tethering us. We're losing it all, all of it, all of this. [Waves gun up and around.] I mean, we're here, you're here, I'm here, we think we're seeing a *movie*, there's a fucking gun, there's a bomb, maybe, and I'm trying to sympathize, right? Or be sympathetic, whatever, and I'm like, "My *calico* died?" [Stops walking, looks around, shocked.] This is my tether, this is how I'm reeling you in? With a dead cat that nobody knows what it is? I mean, what *is* that? What are you supposed to *do* with that? A calico?

Nobody knows what that is. Listen to that, listen to how I'm saying it.

Calico.

Calico.

Flaflingflo.

It's garbage, it's nonsense, nobody knows what to do! There's no connection, we're missing the point, and that's no goddamn good, is it? To miss the point? And no, I hear you, I do, you're like, "We don't want to be *confused*, we want to *understand*." I hear what you're saying, and I'm all throwing fucking *cat names* around? Calico? [Kneels, puts head in hand. Peeks up, sheepishly.] I know what a *black* cat is. Like that makes sense, I know what that is. Like if I said, "My black cat just died." You'd get it, you would, because it's black, and no, and easy, and relax, relax. It is Okay to say black cat, folks. Cats are black, people, some cats are. This is OK, this is part of my declaration, folk, and I'll say it loud and clear.

BLACK CATS!

Wow, listen to that echo, and it's funny, really, it is, it

is. I mean, you're here, right? I'm here. You're being held hostage. The fucking doors? Blow you right the fuck up, you try and walk out, but you're not upset about that. That's not, [Laughs], that's not why you're uncomfortable. That's not why you have that sinking feeling, ma'am. That's not why you're upset right now. It's not all of that, no, it's *"did he just say he knew what a black cat was?"* All clenched teeth. My lord. And folks, I'm going to stop here for a second and warn you. This is another trigger warning, a black cat trigger warning. [Recoils, mock horror.] Can you say black cat trigger? If we're going to be honest here, if we're going to declare, right? If this is going to be an evening of romantic declaring or whatever the hell it says out there, then you are going to have to get your priorities straight. Pull yourselves together.

Chapter Five
The Fixing of a Broken Thing

So, yeah, so no, that's my New Year's Resolution, that's what I'm going to do. Like I *resolve* to do that, whatever I was talking about before. I declare and resolve. And I say I declare sometimes like an old Southern gentlemen, like an old cartoon chicken.

I say eye dee-clay-uh. Like that. I have a fat friend who says I éclair. It's because he's fat, you see ma'am, and he likes éclairs. He likes to eat them. That's not nice, is it? I'm alienating you, aren't I? This isn't relatable anymore? I can add, though, let me think, let me think. [Scratches head, scratches belly.]

Okay, let me throw *this* at you, ma'am. I remember my I-think-ex-wife and I were going to couples therapy, and what happened? [Looks around startled, looks around alarmed.]

Why am I *doing this*? This is what I'm doing? [Looking

around, looking around.] And no, we were going to couples therapy right before we were going to get divorced.
We were getting divorced, it was done, that decision was
made, but the court said before you *do* that, you have to
do this. You have to go to this couples therapy/marriage
counseling type thing. We *had* to do this and to *me*, and
I'm really just thinking about this right now, ma'am,
thinking out loud and that's why I'm laughing. To *me*,
when you're going to get a divorce and the court says,
yeah, before you do that, you've got to go sit with your
soon-to-be-ex and talk about everything another time,
and you do, you go and you dredge up all these awful
feelings and horrible things about your marriage, and
it's awful and brutal and painful and horrible? *That's* the
same thing as when a pregnant woman goes in to get an
abortion and they make her get an ultrasound and listen
to it and look at it. Like at this point, we're just trying
to shame you, you know? Isn't that what this seems like,
ma'am? Right? That we're just trying to hurt your feelings
and make you feel bad? We're piling on, we're morbidly
obese? We don't really expect something to *happen*, right?
Some change, some reconciliation? Some fixing of a broken thing? No, we're just like, yeah, you know what? I'm
just going to stick this to you.

Wow.

That is so *mean!*

Anyway, that happened, my I-guess-ex-wife and I did

this, and who knows what happened, like I'm not, we're not getting into or going into details or specifics here, but all I know is I didn't really get to say a lot of stuff and my ex-wife cried and screamed a lot. That much I do know and can say happened. And we were still living together at that time, like in the same house, and we were getting ready to leave and the therapist said, "Do you have any questions?"

The therapist said do you have any questions and I said, yeah, I have a question. What do I do now? And she said, "Well, you can work on your listening and on being a better this and that," and I said, "No, no, what am I supposed to do *now*, like *right* now? Like we're going to leave here. You're going to say goodbye and maybe see you next week, and we're going to go into a car together, she and I are. She is going to be next to me, I am going to be driving, and it will be cold and night outside, and what am I supposed to do now? What do I do now? Right now, not in some vague future where I work on my whatever, huh-uh. What about right now, like what do I do, do I *look* at her? Shake her hand? Do I cry? Do I say I know, I know. I'm sorry? If I only I would have, maybe we still can? What do I do, I need to know *this*. This is important and I need to know things like this. I can't worry about being a more receptive person, I mean I'm not saying I don't need to be or anything, I'm saying that is so far down the line from what I'm talking about,

I'm talking about *now*, like what do I do *now*. In the next five seconds." This is what I asked, ma'am, this was the only thing that could help me. This was the only thing I wanted to know. And she couldn't answer that question, ma'am, she did not know.

And it's so quiet.

Chapter Six

Something Goes Wrong, Horribly Wrong

So that's a little bit about me, that right there is, and it's sad, isn't it? I mean, I *declare*, you know? So sad, and what that does is, I think, is progress the narrative, right? It moves things forward, it's one more thing accounted for, which is good, I guess, but I don't know if that's necessary. Is it? Is this something I should declare, is this *germane* to the story, ma'am? Is it *germane*, would you tell me if it was *germane*? Have we reached that level of mutual understanding where you would tell me if something was germane? In our relationship? Hostage and hostage-taker? In this evening of romantic lovemaking?

Prior and adjacent to?

Concurrent with?

And these are all things, right? And yes, yes you're being held hostage. I get that, I do, I get it.

Do you *want* to be here?

I don't know, you *came* here, right? And this is the way I see it, this is the way I see it. I put something up on the marquee that said An Evening of Romantic Lovemaking. That's it. That's all I put. And I put the time.

Seven. Put the letters up there myself. Used that big claw thing, grabbed the letters, a number, slapped it right the fuck up there.

Seven.

Seems like a good time, right? I mean, for an evening of romantic lovemaking? Should kick off around seven, right? I mean, that sounds right but to *me?* Seven's a little *late?* It sounds a little late. I like to go to bed early, but not you people. No, sir. No sir, and no ma'am. No, you all showed up, showed up for an evening of romantic lovemaking, and so here you are. So let's get into it. [Puts gun in back of pants, rubs hands together.] All right, it's February, right? How about it? It's the shortest month, Black History Month. These two things are not related, they're not, let's settle down.

February is short.

It is Black History Month.

It is *both* of those things. A thing can be one thing and another thing, ma'am, they can. It's quite possible, it happens all the time. It happened just the other day, he said, setting up a story, I declare. February means that about all our New Year's Resolutions are done, right? We're done with them? Fuck it? Right? Not gonna learn Spanish, not gonna lose weight, not doing it. I got shingles, yeah, just recently. It wasn't a New Year's Resolution. You know what shingles are?

Hurts!

Like hell! I didn't know what it was when I got them. I thought I was having complete renal failure. You ever do that, you ever think you're having complete renal failure? I would have mentioned this to my then-wife, any of this, all of this, but she left. Left and took the kids. Snatched them up like a dimpled Episcopalian, which is the name of a detective book I read or made up just now. The Case of the Dimpled Episcopalian. [Looks out.] Ma'am, is that something? "Snatched up like a dimpled Episcopalian?" Doesn't matter, not why we're here.

That's not this. [Shakes head, waves gun.]

This is locks on doors.

This is barricades.

This is fortified, this is a siege. This is an assault. That's what this is supposed to be, it's supposed to be an assault. Right? Hatches are being battened down as we speak. I've battened them, I have. Ma'am, if the question is "what are the hatches in here like?" If you're like, "What's the hatch-sitch?" If that's what you're asking?

Uh . . . battened?

Battened, would be my response.

Battened! What else is battened, besides hatches? Anybody? And this is serious, this if for real. I'm asking. You don't batten anything else, do you?

Battened about?

Battered? Did somebody say battered? Can you say battered? Stuff like *beer-battered*, that's fun.

That's like fish, ma'am. A fish could be beer-battered, sir. You could batter it with beer. You could get drunk and punch your wife, that's uh, what is that, beer battery?

Can you say that . . . can you make jokes about *domestic abuse*?

Domestic abuse.

We used to call it wife beating. I shouldn't say *we*. It's not like you and I did that, sir. It's not like I hung out with a bunch of folks who said *wife beating, a lot* but people did. Let me see if I can explain this, ma'am. It was called wife beating because you beat your wife, you beat her. You beat her about the face and neck. I don't know if that's true, like if it was specifically those two areas, that's irrelevant, it is. The point *is*, the relevant thing is, that you beat her. And no, and goddamn it, and I see what you're doing there, I do. No, I am not saying that this is good, that wife beating is. I'm not saying it's great, it isn't, and I never did it, not one time, but that's what we called it, and by we I mean they, and it wasn't great, but it was accurate, the term was. It was accurate and not vague, I can tell you that, I can and I will, and let's see, and what else? Let's Reestablish, let's level-set.

We're here in a movie theater, right?

Lights, camera, action?

And you came to see some movie called *An Evening of*

Romantic Lovemaking? That was the title? And now you're being held hostage? I'd see that movie, I would.

You ever see that movie, I forget the name of it, some science-fiction thing, where some *astronauts*, some *scientists*, they go to space and something goes wrong, terribly wrong? Have you seen that one? Where some astronauts go out into space and something goes wrong, terribly wrong? That's a good one; I like that one.

Did you ever see that *movie* [Voice rising], where there's like a guy and a girl and they don't like each other? They don't like each other, and they get on each other's whatever? And you know, and it's not like they *hate* each other, but they just like *annoy* each other, right? And then the girl, it's something like she takes off her glasses or something and then is good looking and then everybody likes that girl and then that guy that she was annoyed with, they fall in love, you ever see *that* movie? That's a good one, I like that one. That's a little bit about me, that I like that movie. You ever see that action movie where the guy gets revenge on someone who's done him wrong? Ever see that, where a guy, where he gets revenge? Those are all good. You ever see that movie where there's this comedian and he talks about something and you think he's talking about one thing, but in the end he's talking about something else? But it's *kind of* like what he was talking about in the first place, only different? You ever see that one, that movie? That's a good one, that's a good, ah, movie.

So my whole thing is that I don't know what this is or what I'm supposed to be doing here. I mean, I get the part where I've barricaded the doors and nobody can get out. [Looks out, menu-faces.] And are we still going with that, is that still the premise? The assumption that we're operating under here? And I'll be honest with you, I never, I never liked that, I never thought that was any *good*. Because, how'm I, because it's not *plausible*, you know? Because this whole hostage thing? The explosives and the rigging, the aforementioned *rigging?* It's just not something I'd be able to *do*. Like I think it's *clear* that I'm good at *talking* about things, but I'm not good at actually *doing* things. That's *kind* of why I'm here in the first place, isn't it? Why *we're* here? See the *idea*, this whole *idea*, the idea of this whole place, this is good, it's good, but I don't know what to *do*, and I'm not really interested in anything, I'm just interested in the idea, you know?

Words and shapes and sounds.

Arrangement.

That's what I'm interested in. I'm not interested in running a movie theater! What the fuck do I know about that? Taking hostages? Killing a guy? [Stops, looks aside at audience. Quicky wrinkles nose, shakes head.] Come *on*, and what, and could it be that I'm not interested in it because I'm not *good* at it? Like lovemaking, like being a husband? Like being a father to my kids? I don't know, that's possible, I guess, I don't know. And this is not *funny* anymore, is it? This isn't relatable, we're not having fun here, are we? An evening of romantic what-now? Maybe I'll tell a joke. I'll tell some jokes, some more jokes. And don't worry, I'm very *funny* ma'am, I am. I'm not doing it now, like right now, at this part. No, this is the introspective part, where I'm trying to use the narrative to explain something, right? Something like that, that's what's going on? I don't know, I mean, maybe, right? Tough to say. But here's a joke that I heard.

What do you tell a woman with two black eyes?

[Stops, eyes wide, sucks air through clenched teeth.]

Oh, *that's* not good!

We're already uncomfortable here, aren't we? [Leans in, crouches.] But seriously, what do you tell a woman with two black eyes? [Stands up, wipes pretend dust off legs. Looks out. Smiles.]

Nothing. [Pauses, cups gun hand to ear.]

And it's so quiet.

Unless it's the name of a place where she can go and get some help. That's what you tell her. And you thought it was going to go one way, but it went another way, and that's what I was talking about earlier, about how things can be two things, or a thing can be a thing and also another thing. Or one thing can be a thing and another thing can be another thing. I *think* that's what I was saying, I think, before. And I'm not *comfortable* talking about battered wives. And I understand, you're like, "That's odd."

[Looks out, nods slowly.]

Look at you, sir. [Points with gun hand.]

You're like, "That's odd, because what you've done here, is you've taken people hostage and you've forced them to listen to your act, right? Your declaration. Your evening of romantic lovemaking."

And that's a great title, let's get back to that for a second. Forget about all this for a second. [Waves arms up and around.]

Forget about the hostages, right.

Forget about the impending bankruptcy.

Forget about the loss of love, forget about the divorce. About the losing everything, about the squandering opportunities, forget about being disgraced and besmirched. The dead dog. My poor dog.

I want a new dog, ma'am [Pacing again]. When this is done, when this is all over? If I make it? Then I want a new dog, I do, I do. Huey Lewis wanted a new *drug*, but I want a new *dog*. He wanted a new drug, but I want a new dog. I'm not saying I don't want the drug, and I'm not saying I would or wouldn't take it, but let's pause, let's pause. Let's hit pause on this right now. This is beside the point, this is not "to the point," and we're getting sidetracked here. So, dogs. I want a new dog, so I'm looking at different dogs, right? What kind of dog do you *get*, right? Do you get short-hair dog or long-hair dog? Do you keep it inside or does it go *out*side, you know? Do

you walk it around a lot, does it spin and turn? Is it an
Australian Spinner? A Brazilian Turn-Sitter? Is that it, the
kind of dog, is that the one? A Shetland Roundheel? A
Corgi? I don't know, there's a lot of variables and factors,
and what I have to do, what I have to do as a conscien-
tious person, a thoughtful person, a person who puts a lot
of thoughts into actions, I have to look at my situation
and determine which dog is best, best for me. So that is
what I did, ma'am, I did that, I did *just* that and I'm like
I *know* I want a couple of things, in this dog, right? Like I
know, I've got kids, or used to, so I want something that's
good with kids, that's important, so that's a criteria. I want
it to be *good* with kids, but I also want it to be deadly.
[Looks out, stone-faced.] Like I want it to be good with
the kids, on the off chance that I (a) make it out of here
alive and (b) am allowed to see my kids ever again. I want
that, but I also want it to be super deadly. Like I *want it*,
hmm, how do I best say this? [Hand on head, thinking.]
    Like I *want* it to be good with kids, *but* I'd also like it
to be able to *kill*, you know? I want it to be able to just
kill things, quickly. That would be nice, a nice feature in a
dog. I like options, folks. Dog options. So to summarize,
the dog, again, needs to be good with kids yet deadly.
You're thinking a Cobradoodle, am I right? Like I'll get
one of those, a Cobradoodle [Shrugs shoulders, lowers
mic, tilts head].
    It's a dog with some doodle in it.

Peekadoodle?

Pockadoodle?

Something, right, who cares? It's a doodle! Yay, it's fun! So you got that, right, it's like a dog, like the doodle part, but then also a cobra.

A cobra!

Now *that's* a dog, right there! And I'm thinking, okay so jump cut to me having owned a Cobradoodle for a while. I have a Cobradoodle and it's been around for I don't know, a few years and the question is what's it like? The question, sir, is what is it like to own a Cobradoodle, what's the best part? I say the *best* part when I look back, and this is kind of surprising, but the best part about owning a Cobradoodle is that you don't have to spend a lot of money on grooming. That's the best part because their fur is, you know what their fur's like, sir, don't scowl. You know what a Cobradoodle's fur is like, they don't have any, and so, yeah, so the best part is that you don't have to spend a lot on grooming, that's the best part.

And the *worst part* is that it spits venom in your face. That's the *worst*.

Oh my God!

The spitting? Ma'am, honestly? It's terrible. Like that's the worst part by far! And I'm seriously trying to think here, like what's worse than when a Cobradoodle spits venom in your face, and I'm like *nothing*. Nothing is worse than that. Clearly.

And now I'm being serious here, but what seriously could be worse than that, like that's the worst thing that a Cobradoodle could do, what else could it be? Would it be worse if he was always late to things? That's bad, but spitting venom in the face? That's the worst. Is that what we're agreeing on, here? I mean, no one's going to say it *isn't* bad. The only question is if it's the worst, true? Like if I said, and this is interesting, ma'am, hold on, hold that thought.

But I know your objection. You could object that, well, what if what the dog were spitting in my face was really an antidote to a venom that was already in me? That could happen. Perhaps the Cobradoodle thinks he's saving me. Like Lassie. Dogs sense things we don't, you know. Maybe venom is one, but what I'm saying first of all is that that probably wouldn't happen? Like that wouldn't *happen*, because how would the dog know which antidote to use?

And you're like, well, what about if the venom wasn't really *venom*, and I'm like, yeah, but it is venom. That's the whole premise here, sir and ma'am. The premise is that this dog that is good with the kids also on occasion spits venom in my face.

So, I think you're getting confused here. I'm not talking, I'm not talking about the *idea* of venom. I'm talking about actual venom, empirical venom. I am saying it is bad to spit venom in somebody's face, especially if you're a pet dog, the family pooch. This seems like a simple thing to say and not something we can argue about. We're not arguing about venom, are we? Venom, ma'am? An eve-venoming? Isn't this a hostage situation? What does this have to do with anything? But let's assume that you're here, right? Anyway, and these are clues, right? Clues and hints from a detective story I'd write if I knew how, but that's not what we're talking about, so forget about that!

Forget about that!

It's not *important*!

You know what's *important*? At the end of the *day*? What's important is that it's a good title. It's a *great* title! The name of a thing!

An Evening of Romantic Lovemaking.

Look at that! Lit up on the marquee! My God, that marquee is beautiful, it really is. I will miss it, I will. I'd describe it, tell you what it looks like, say it reminds me of this or makes me think of that, but you know what it looks like. I'm not just saying that because I have a hard time describing things, even though I do. Terrible at it. I can't describe how things look or how people act or feel. I can't say how I feel, can't explain anything if I wanted to, but no, that *title?*

I'm in.

Chapter Seven

Signified and Roy

Full disclosure, folks, full transparency, I'm not good at
making love. I'm not. In fact, I'm terrible at it. Probably
why I said I wasn't interested in it, earlier. Makes sense?
That one thing would lead to another thing? We could
draw a chart, a diagram; anybody got a pen? No, but I'm
not good at it, you can ask anybody. Well, not *anybody*.
Like if you asked this guy? [Points with gun.] He wouldn't
know, I don't think, so just go ahead and take my word
for it. This is trust, this is you relying on me. This is you
believing me when I say I'm not good. No *bueno*. I'd like
to say, "Oh this is a relatively new, you know, develop-
ment, the me being terrible at lovemaking is."

I'd like to say it's the stress, ma'am.

I'd like to say it's the pressures, ma'am.

Maybe cancer? [Eyebrows up, quizzical.] Maybe
the maybe-cancer? That makes sense, right? That the

maybe-cancer started this, that's the origin. From this, that. From this, [Points mic at chest] that. [Points at crowd with gun.] And I've got a little secret I'm going to share with you, something real. [Crouches down, looks side to side, stage-whispers.] *I'm not sure this place gave me cancer.* [Smiles, stands back up, pacing.] Like maybe I had it already? Maybe I was already dying? Maybe there was something already? Something inside? Rotting like an otter, a tumor-otter? An otter-tumor? And what's the deal with music, today, am I right ma'am, what with all the otter-tumor? And in all honesty, I am pretty sure everybody has cancer. Do you, ma'am? Have cancer? Seems like everybody does. It's everywhere, isn't it? In the air, in the food, the water, in the everything, and we do it to ourselves, don't we? Like those things you stick in your ears, those air things? [Looks pleadingly into crowd.] Ma'am, help me out here, I'm exhausted, I am. [Puts head down, shoulders slumped, defeated.] I'm tired and no good at making love, I've said this, I'm explaining this. Full disclosure, a declaration, an accounting, and what's that? [Looks up, looks out, menu-faces.] Say that again, ma'am? [Listening, hearing, smiling.]

AIRPODS!

YES!

Thank you, ma'am. See? You get it! You and me, ma'am. [Taps chest with gun, points gun out at crowd. Looks at gun, wrinkles nose and shakes head.] Anyway,

AirPods, beginning of a bit, and this cancer, it's in the air. Those air pods you have? That you stick in your ears and they wirelessly transmit shit? That's not giving you cancer? And let's be honest, it's KIND OF WORTH IT, isn't it? Shouldn't that be the slogan for those things, "AirPods: Kind of Worth the Brain Cancer"? Because let's face it, ma'am, let's be honest, let's hash it out, isn't it? Let's look at it clearly, even though it's so dark in here? These AirPods, right? You stick them in your ears, and they're like headphones, except they're tiny, aren't they? And you cram them in your ears, right? Cram them and jam them and you can hear your music or whatever. You can tap one of them and then it will play the next song. You can tap the *other* one and then, and here's the funny part, ma'am, you can tap the *other* one and you can ask it *any question in the world* and it will answer you!

It will give you the answer!

You can tap your head and go, "What's rack and pinion steering?"

And it will tell you!

How many pints in a quart?

It will tell you!

What's a yard and a pint?

SAME THING!

ANSWERS!

RESOLUTION!

I DECLARE! And that right there, ma'am? That's not

worth a little brain cancer? A smattering? [Pauses, smirks, waves hands all around.] You thought this was *free*? You thought this wasn't going to *cost anything*? I told you I spent a million dollars here, didn't I? I lost everything, kids, wife, money. Got cancer, fucking *otter cancer*, sir, but it's a trade-off, that's what this is. You want this, you have to give that. This is physics, this is matter. This is a thing having consequences. These are ramifications. My mom's mother had grandmafications. Here's a great story, ma'am. It's one I like a lot. I'm not sure what it has to DO with anything, but I'll tell it anyway.

A little bit about me. I like to ride my bike. I do. Keeps me fit, keeps me svelte. I like to get up early in the morning and ride. When it's cold outside, I ride inside. I have what's called a trainer. You ever hear of that, sir? A trainer? Ever hear of a trainer? It's nothing really. You hook your bike up to it and you can ride. Anyway, I got up the other day and I was going to ride. It was like 3 A.M. And what I like to DO is, I like to read books while I ride, detective books, ma'am. Lou books. I like the solving of the thing. I always have. Anyway, I ride and I read detective books, but sometimes I don't. Sometimes I watch movies. I watch them on my TV, I watch them on my phone, whichever. Sometimes both. The other day was one of those times. I got up and was going to go ride and I started watching this movie on my phone. I was drinking coffee, drinking water, getting ready to

ride. I hooked up my bike to the trainer. [Quick look
out.] We've established what a trainer is? We're good with
that? Anyway, bike hooked up, movie going, pedal pedal.
Watching the movie and I realize something. I'm alone.
Then-wife gone, kids gone. Dog dead. I am all alone. It
is so quiet, ma'am. So quiet in my dark and empty house.
There is nobody in this house, and it dawns on me. I
don't have to watch on my phone, I can turn the TV up!
Loud and clear, ma'am! A victory! Lemons and lemonade,
right, so fuck it, I say, except I really didn't, and I quick
grab the remote from the table next to me, still pedaling
by the way, ma'am! No wasted effort! And I'm pedaling
and I'm turning the TV on because why not, right? And
the Apple TV logo comes on and I'm about ready to
switch over to Netflix to continue the movie I was watching on the phone, and the TV says "Updates Available for
Download." [Pauses.] You ever see that, ma'am? You ever
see a sign that says "Updates Available for Download"?
[Leans in, quick look from side to side like he doesn't
want to be overheard.] What we're doing right now is
RELATING. [Points to chest with gun, points out at
audience, points back at chest. Smiles, stands up.] So
the sign is asking, I think, if I want something to update,
and of course I do, right, so I use another remote that is
sitting there and click Yes.

Yes, I want to update, I am declaring. This is something I want to do. So I click Yes and the screen goes

black. The apple logo fills the screen along with a tiny
progress bar at the bottom. It is slowly filling up grey. You
know exactly what this is. I can't describe the marquee, I
can't tell you the sick sinking feeling I feel when I think
about my boys being gone, but when I say the gray line at
the bottom of the screen? Totally get you. [Laughs, wipes
tears from eye.] So there I am. I'm riding, pedaling, in
the dark. Did I mention I was in the dark? That I was in
my basement at three in the morning, pedaling in the
dark, going nowhere? Is that important, is that germane?
Well, of course I'm in the dark, ma'am? If I'm watching
a movie? You're about to watch a movie, aren't you? *An
Evening of Romantic Something or Other*? Lovemaking?
Isn't that what we're pretending is happening? YOU'RE
in the dark, aren't you? So it just makes sense, right?
Anyway, I'm in the dark pedaling, the screen is updating, it's downloading, or whatever, and it is quiet, quiet.
All I hear is the hum and thrush of my bike. Wheels
spinning, and I think what if. I think what if I go back
on my phone, right? Jam those cancer buds back in my
ears and keep watching the movie on Netflix like I was
in the beginning, right? Always thinking! So that's what I
do. I plug them in my ears, I tap a couple of things, and
voilà, MOVIE TIME! So I keep watching the movie and
I look at the TV again and it's still updating. It's about
half done, maybe a little more than half. I'm not good
at guessing. I may have said this already. Anyway, it's

still updating, and I'm thinking, "What is it DOING," you know? And how is it doing it? Beams and particles. Waves transmitted and information sent and I am pedaling, you know? In the dark, watching another thing on a smaller screen and waves and particles are being sent and received. And I have no idea how this is happening, and I don't know anybody who does. Nobody I know would be able to explain this thing that we all understand, you know? And I'm alone and there is nobody here that I can ask. My then-wife, my boys, my dog, and I'm pedaling and watching the movie and then it's done. The update is over. Whatever was supposed to happen has happened. There is a finality, ma'am, except everything kind of looks the same, and I'm pedaling, I'm riding, I'm sweating, and I'm watching the movie on my phone and I'm about to stop and start the movie on the OTHER screen, because why not, right, and right then? Right then I start wondering if when I start watching the movie on the BIG screen, the movie that I was just watching on the little phone screen, what if I have to rewind or something? Like go back to where I had started it on the big screen. Because of the updates, right? Like would it pick up on the big screen right where I left off on the little screen? And there is anticipation here, ma'am, right? This is big, right? This is this morning, this is earlier today, this whole thing was, and I'm sitting there, I'm riding there, and I'm using the remote for the Apple TV to get Netflix going, and I do, and I'm riding, and the movie comes up, and I click it. And it says Resume or Start Over and I click resume. And I'm pedaling, ma'am, heart racing, and it PICKS UP RIGHT WHERE THE PHONE LEFT OFF! There is a continuation, there is progress! Nothing has changed, nothing interrupted! This is a miracle, and they happen every day, ma'am! And I'm pedaling and I'm watching and I am alone, alone with all this majesty, all this wonder, and I think if I told my grandma this? Like if I recounted this whole scene about the Netflix and the updates and the Apple TV and the seamless transition? If I recounted it like I just did now? The only thing she'd say was, "You ride a bike INSIDE?"

And that's a great story, I think, but yeah, I'm not sure what it has to do with anything. [Looks out, confused.]

Does it fit?

I don't know . . . maybe it does. I'm not sure how that fits into whatever it is I'm supposed to be doing, but that's not my decision, is it? I'm supposed to make a full and complete accounting, to declare, and if that's what I'm supposed to be doing, if those are my instructions, then maybe I'm doing exactly what I'm supposed to be doing. In that case, this makes sense.

But then again, how much sense can I be making here? I've got like ten minutes before the fucking cops show up and I've got to get all this out. I'm kind of surprised it's lasting this long, to tell you the truth. I'd assumed there'd be guns and badges and smoke. My hatches, ma'am. My aforementioned hatches. [Laughs, wipes eyes. Clears throat.] I suppose I should tell you there's a trigger warning here, like something that might upset you? Is that right? That's what we're doing now? You're supposed to say there's a trigger warning so people can know, like in advance, right? That there's something coming that might upset you, right? This seems fair? Is this something I should have done? Like at the beginning?

Where was *my* trigger warning, ma'am? The one that said, "Hey, maybe don't do this? Don't do any of this, any of what you're about to do?" [Quick nod of head.] I didn't get a warning, I got *encouraged!* They egged me on, ma'am, they did, they did. Like an otter in a zoo, ma'am, that's how much they egged me. You know that old expression? "Egged like an otter at a zoo?" This is something people say, right? To each other, under certain circumstances? Trigger, please! [Stops, smiles.] Come on, that's funny, we're having fun here, right? I declare, I declare, yeah but no, in this case, I guess, it's an actual trigger that I'm warning you about, a trigger that's attached to a gun that I'm going to use to blow your head off if you try and leave here. [Points gun at audience. Laughs.] No, but seriously, you see what I'm saying? So that, [Looks at gun] this, is an actual trigger warning. This is a thing that is aligning with the actual thing, right? Signified and signifier and all that. Signified and Roy, and that's a good thing, right? An omen, a portent? Things aligning, and what's the actual warning, I'm wondering? [Stops, scratches head with gun.] You ever do that, ma'am? You ever wonder about the warning? Ever do a little warning-wonder? [Smiles, gives quick nod to crowd.] *This* guy gets it! Look at you, sir! You may be my only friend right now! No, but seriously, what's the actual warning, here? Is it the trigger? You want me to warn you about the trigger? I can do that. I don't feel comfortable saying "*trigger*." [Scrunches face disgustedly. Quick shake of head.] Like I don't feel this is something I should be saying.

Trigger?

Ma'am?

No, you can't say that, can you?

Trigger?

One time I was driving and there was a Black lady and she was walking in the middle of the street, like crossing in the middle of the road, and she was walking into a Kentucky Fried Chicken, into a Kentucky Fried Segue, into a Kentucky Fried What Is He Doing? [Stops. Smiles.]

A Kentucky Fried This Is Uncomfortable, and I know, but no, she was. That is exactly what was happening, the scene I am describing now, the one I just did. And I said to myself out loud, I said, "There's a Black lady walking across the street going to a Kentucky Fried Chicken." And I said this out loud, in my car, and then I said, "Is that racist?" [Looks out, menu-faces.]

Not to *her*, ma'am, she couldn't hear me, but to me. [Taps gun on chest.] I said it to me, I said is that racist, because it isn't, ma'am. It was exactly what was happening.

Facts are, ma'am.

Black woman, ma'am.

Crossing in middle of street, sir.

Entering Kentucky Fried Chicken, your Honor.

I declare, I declare.

And I have no idea how this is helping, but that's *exactly* what she was doing, *exactly* what was happening. My recounting. Events thereof.

That's not racist, that's exactly what happened, and it's so quiet, isn't it? [Puts gun hand to lips, makes *shhhh* motion.]

It's so quiet right now.

Chapter Eight

The Shit and the Rubble
and the Maybe Carburetors

[Sighs deeply, laughs.]

But damn it, I'm going to miss this place, I am. I mean, look around. It's beautiful. And you know how bad this was before, right? When I got it? You saw this in the papers, right, that whole story? The state it was in?

Disheveled?

Is that what you said, ma'am, "disheveled"?

Jesus, I *wish*!!

How about "complete fucking disaster"?

How about "can't see two feet in front of your face"?

How about shit everywhere, how about fucking histoplasmosis and asbestos and every other goddamn thing?

I would've *killed* for disheveled, ma'am! [Looks out quickly, shakes head.]

Not literally, folks, at ease, at ease. You knew this, right? I was in the paper and on TV all the time back then.

"Look at him go!" the paper said.

"He is really doing a lot of work in there!" the TV said.

"What a great thing he is doing for the community! I hope his wife doesn't leave him and take his three boys!" the radio said, and there would be interviews of me and articles of me and pictures of me. I would be lifting out rubble, carting out, wheelbarrows full. Throwing it into dumpsters. In and out, ma'am, the old in and out, all day. [Stops, raises eyebrows, gun hand covering mouth.]

And *all night*, perhaps?

And see, [Looks down, brow furrowed, thinking] this is fun, and here's the part where I could tell a story about what happened back when I first got here. This would be good, it would. Establishing, and whatnot. Relatable, and forthwith. Declaring, and here's a story, here's something, and you'll like this one, you will. It's about otters, which is fun. [Looks out, holds mic out to crowd.]

Who's in?

Show of hands? [Pretends to count.]

No, I'm just kidding, I can't see any of you anyway, I'm going to go ahead and tell it anyway.

What if, [Crouches down] and I'm asking now, you can tell by the way my voice just went up, *what if* there was this guy who bought this movie theater, this building,

okay? Just a guy, just a building, right, and what if when
he *did*, what if there was all kinds of stuff everywhere?
[Gets up, starts walking.] It was run down, the building
was, condemned, contaminated, infested. It was full of
debris, and shit—real shit, bird shit, raccoon shit—and
pipe organs, and parts, and machinery, and paint cans,
and rubble, and maybe carburetors. I think they were
carburetors. I don't know, do you? I mean, would you,
ma'am, know what a carburetor looks like? [Stopping,
staring, pleading.] Would you know what a *lot of them*
looked like? Do you know what a movie theater looks
like? Seats and a stage? Like an old-time one? This place,
this stage, was like that, full of *everything*. Everything
you can think of, ma'am, and I mean this, right? Because
there was everything in here, ma'am, I saw it. I saw it
because I was here. Everything in the world was there.

And so, and anyway, and what if, and what if.

And what if there was a day when it made sense. Like
all of it? All of the mess and clutter and jumble and pipe
organs and maybe carburetors and filth and disease and
rubble made sense? Not like it made sense, no, and I'm
wrong, and I'm pacing, and I'm scratching my head. I
mean it made sense in the sense that what if the guy just
decided all he had to do was *move that stuff*? [Stopping,
smiling.] Like accepting, right? Accepting and acknowl-
edging and yes, this is daunting, yes this is going to be
hard. Yes, you will want to quit and yes, this may kill you,

but you could do it. Just move that stuff out, and then he could start. Start building, start making, start lights-camera-actioning. There was something here, an idea, a thing, right? A pure thing, a kernel, a core, buried in the shit and the rubble and the maybe carburetors. Maybe carburetors, maybe cancer, but there were a lot of other things too, additional things you had to get out. You had to get all of these other some-things out first, right? All of this stuff. [Waving arms, looking around.] All of this stuff just had to get out of here. The pipe organs, the boxes, the logs, the pigeons. The seats and the hats and the bricks and the pieces of wall. Move it out. And so that's what he did, ma'am, he meaning me, we started moving. And you couldn't see, and I've said that, in there. You couldn't see anything just like I can't see you now. You couldn't see anything, that's how much stuff, and ask me how much stuff, ma'am, go ahead. Say how much stuff was in there. I'll wait. There was just *so* much. And on that day, that first day, he cleared a path, didn't move anything out really, just cleared a path. A path to the stage, this stage. And after a few more days, he could walk on stage. That was a big day, wasn't it? When that happened? I declare! And I know, right, that you weren't there, none of you were or are. I know this, but I'm telling you it was because I was there then like I'm here now, here, and on this stage, the one I'm talking about, the one it took a day to *get to*, to reach, ma'am. [Voice forceful, index finger pointing at crowd.]

And there was this huge cabinet. And that's not the right word, cabinet, because you're thinking something that it isn't, you're thinking of something small, a kitchen cabinet, I can tell, I can see. I've lost you, haven't I? [Stopping, head tilted, looking down.] In the middle of all this stuff, [Quickly looking up] this stuff that isn't majesty, ma'am, not yet, not yet, we're not there yet. Because in my head, [Pointing to head] I know what this is, this big cabinet that isn't really a cabinet. I can see it, and I don't know if I can see it because I *saw* it, or because it's a thing that exists, you know, some sort of empirical thing-that-looks-like-a-cabinet-but-isn't. This cabinet is as tall as the ceiling [Speaking softly, hushed, reverential] and it goes up as far as it goes, and it's as wide as the stage itself and it took days and days to get to it, to move all of the organ pipes and chairs and pigeons, to get to a point where you could *walk* to the stage and *stand* on it and see the cabinet in its majesty, can you imagine? And can you imagine? And seriously, and I'm being serious here, *are there bathrooms in this place?* Do you have them, ma'am, is what I'm asking?

[Raises himself up, smiling.]

And this cabinet? It's chicken-wired. [Quick look down.] Ma'am, do you know chicken wire? Do you know it if I say it like it's a verb, like it's chicken-wired?

A gerund? Thank you, sir, very helpful. [Makes a snide face, sneers.] This fucking guy.

"A gerund." [Shakes head.]

Anyway, it's all sealed? Does this, do these, does any?

Was the cabinet being protected? Is that what I'm pretending somebody said? I guess. It's protected, yeah, because there are things in there, maybe valuable things, and pan out a little, can we? Just back this up a little so you can see the whole shot, an establishing shot [Looking over shoulder at audience]. Is that, did you? I think that's right, so take that and look and see where we are. There's a guy in a huge, abandoned room that is full of everything, bits of everything and there is a tiny path to a stage and on that stage is a big cabinet and that cabinet is wired shut. Do you see this? [Looking up, looking out, eyes wide, smiling, hoping.] You see this, right?

So, what if what happens, [Walks slowly backward, framing scene with hands, eyes wide] what if what happens is that he cuts all the wire? With bolt cutters, sir. Did he find them there? Did he find the bolt cutters in the middle of all that mess? Ooh, that's good, it is! Did he find them in betwixt and between the mud and the asbestos and the hair and the pipe organs and the seats and the engine parts and the soot and the rubble and the dead pigeon disease? Maybe. I mean, and I'm thinking out loud now, that would make it better, right? It would be better if I said something like he used something *out* of that mess to create some kind of *order*, right?

To cut through, to assemble, to organize? Do you see

where I'm going with this? Can you even see me any-more? I'm still here, right? [Quick laugh, continues to walk.] Let's say that happened, that he used a thing from the mess to help clean that mess. Makes sense, seems to fit. So he's cutting the wire from the cabinet, floor to ceiling, end to end, and it's filled. The cabinet is filled, ma'am, on stage, top to bottom, chicken-wired shut. And what does this mean? This means that in the middle of this [Waving arms] somebody thought, "I need to protect all this." Right? [Laughing.] And the reason I'm laughing is because I'm right, I have to be. Because here are the facts and facts are things you have to have here. If you're going to try and make sense out of any of this, you're going to have to understand that in the middle of all this, some-body tried to make some order. That's what I thought then and that's what I think now. Somebody had taken something and put it in a cabinet, sealed it up, ma'am.

Anyway you look at it, somebody, Somebody, *pro-tected* it. Kept it safe. So naturally I opened it. Had to, right? Didn't I have to open it? [Voice raised, squinting out into light.] I was like Harrison Ford or I was like the Nazis with the Ark of the Covenant. I was a raider. And it's tough, I can't really see your face, but I can tell you're saying *did you*? Did you have to open this? I did, ma'am, and guess what was in there?

Chapter Nine
Brazil Nuts

And look at that! Look at what we did just there! Just there and then! We were *in it*, weren't we? We were *invested!* [Smiling, laughing, waving gun around.] That's narrative progression, ma'am, that's what that is. We were all together, all of us. That's romantic lovemaking, sir, I declare! And what was in it? Shit, doesn't matter, does it? Because this is all going away, all of it. This is all going. Going, going, gone, and I should probably explain this, but I'm not going to. And there's a reason for this, why I'm not going to explain this and the reason I'm not going to explain this is because I'm not going to explain myself.

Tomorrow?

Tomorrow, I've got to declare, I do. But that's tomorrow, ma'am, tomorrow and not today and unless you're some sort of time traveler? Unless you're, I don't know, some kind of time-travelling Willbury? Then I'm not explaining, not to you, not to me, not to anybody. I'm not going to. I'm done with all the explaining. I can't live like this, like that. I can't and I won't. It hurts, ma'am, explaining does, and that's the truth, I declare.

I made this decision, the decision to not explain myself, when I was still married. We were married, this wife and I were, and we were having fun still, right? [Smiling, looking up at audience.] And I said to her once, I said, "I'm not going to explain myself. If I do something, I'm just not." And I trailed off there when that happened, ma'am . . . like I'm trailing off now . . .

I said this, I said this like that. I said, "I'm not going to explain myself. I'm just going to *do* things." And I didn't really know what I was talking about, ma'am, back then or now, and I'm pointing, pointing. And I was serious, too, that's the thing.

[Looks up, looks out.]

Completely serious about this, about me not explaining myself. This is important to me. I've always been very certain about the things I was very certain about, then and now. I've always believed very strongly in whatever I was believing in at that particular time. Like whatever it was that I was into, I was always *really* into it, *very* into it. And I'd believe it absolutely, whole-heartedly. Extremely. Gary Cherone could not have been, you know, more whole-hearted in his, ah, fanaticism. Ma'am, what I'm saying is, is that my, my dedication, to whatever it was that I was dedicated to has been and *can only be described as* Cheronian in its whole-heartedness. Do you understand [Leans forward, tilts head]? And I don't want to be the kind of guy who throws out, you know, Gary Cherone references lightly because that's not, we're not, I'm not, he's not, they didn't, so, no, it isn't. That's not what this is.

Let me ask you something, and I'm going to level with you. [Stops, face serious, palms outstretched.] Ma'am, do you see me here, can you see me through all this? My palms outstretched, ma'am? [Quick nod of head, quick smile, back walking.] Did you think that this was going to be like one of those things where people were just going to bandy about Cherone-isms? Like Cheronian in the extremity of my enthusiasms? Like willy-nilly, askance, Cherone-ing everything? Here [Stands in center of stage, pointing]? You thought that would happen *here*?

Well, you were Cheronius in that assumption [Laughing] and, oh, my God. That's good, and what're we going to do, seriously though? Like what am *I* going to do and do you ever think about killing yourself? I mean, I know you think about it, but do you *think* about it? You *should*. I thought about it a lot, and of course I did, right? Be silly if I didn't, wouldn't it? I figured I'd just do it and everybody would be better off. Shoot myself in the face, hang myself in the face, didn't matter, either one. I never did, though, ma'am, never did it, unless I did. You laugh, but I'm serious. Serious as a heart attack, as a gun, as maybe-cancer. As a bomb and a door. You know that old expression, that adage? That old chestnut. That old Brazil nut.

Speaking of which, who here has heard the expression "nigger toes"?

[Pauses, looks out.]

What?

Nothing?

[Looks out, arms pleading, into bright light.]

Really. Nothing. I'm supposed to believe that none of you has ever heard the term "nigger toes"? It's just me.

Right, okay, have it your way. [Walking, laughing.] Well then, let me explain, seeing how this is *just me* and *nobody else* has any clue what I'm talking about and this is just a huge fucking mystery. [Sighs, sneers, wipes brow.] You see folks, *nigger toe* is what people used to call a Brazil nut. You know Brazil nuts, ma'am? Can I, is this? A Brazilian *nut*? Is there a connection? Is a light bulb going off anywhere at all? A 40-watt bulb? And I'm just going to stare at you uncomfortably for a while.

[Stands, stares.]

Okay, it was something my grandmother said, "nigger toes." She called them nigger toes, and it's not like this went on a *lot*, ma'am. Let me clarify. It's not like it happened all the time, no. I mean, how often do you think we had Brazil nuts? I mean, seriously. That'd be weird, wouldn't it? No, it's not like we were just [Laughing] eating these Tony Montana-sized mounds of Brazil nuts that were laying around my grandmother's apartment, right? Like there were all these *opportunities* for us to shout "nigger toes" at the little top of our little lungs. [Looks confused.]

Tops of lungs?

Tops of lung? It's confusing, I know it is. It's a fucking mess, the whole thing is. [Shakes head, moves on.] I mean, it came up on occasion, that's all. This is all I am saying, people. That's it. It was a thing I heard her say, people say.

In fact, I was just mentioning it the other day at home. I was saying something about my grandmother, and I guess that triggered something, you know? Trigger toes, so I said to my then-wife, I said, "Hey, did you ever call those nuts 'nigger toes'?" [Looks down at crowd.] I feel like I can tell you people this, and not just because you're being held hostage and you fear for your lives. It's not that, it isn't. I mean, it's *kind of that*? Like it's partially because of [Nods at gun] and you know the doors, but it's more than that, I think. I feel safe with you people, I do, I declare, but no, but I said that and my then-wife was like, "What?" Shocked, right? Shocked! "What are you *saying*?" Because I'd said, you know . . . *n-toes*, ma'am.

N-word toes, ma'am.

Something that rhymed with *trigger toes*, ma'am.

Right, but I was *mad* though, right then I was. Like *I* was the one who invented that! I hadn't ma'am, *and if you're insinuating,* ma'am!

Voice raised, ma'am!

Italicized fonts, ma'am!

No, but it was a *thing*, a saying, I was sure of that even if no one else would admit it. And so I thought, "Fuck it" you know, I'm going to look it up. That's what I thought, I thought fuck this, I'm going to look up "n-toes" on my phone. [Stops, thinks.] And that's funny, it is, that I felt fine saying eff but not enn. [Stares.] So I did. And ma'am, you know Google. You know it? The search engine? [Pause. Smiles.] That'd be funny. Next time somebody says Google, says they're going to Google something, be like, "Google the search engine?"

I'm going to Google feudalism.

You mean like Google, the search engine?

What? Yeah.

Ok, that's what I . . .

What *other* Google would I be thinking of?

What?

I mean, you said, "Google the search engine," like why would you, what other Google would it be?

What?

What other Google *but* the search engine Google would make sense if I said I'm going to Google feudalism? Like how does that even make *sense*?

Yeah, no, that's why I asked.

[Laughs.] Yeah, do that, do that. I didn't, but that's what I did. [Looks out, smiles.] And you know what happens, ma'am, when you type in N on the ol' Google? It starts spitting it out, doesn't it?

Spitting it *out!*

NBA, Netflix, NASCAR!

N's!

N-words!

Nacogdoches!

Nickels!

N!

Helpful!

And I type NA and it goes nails, narwhal, Nantucket, everything!

Natchez, nature, Nat King Cole, cole slaw!

Helpful!

And I type NAN because I hit the wrong key, but Google doesn't know that, doesn't know I made a mistake, right? This is just math happening. [Types on gun like it's a phone.] It sees these letters and is operating under some algorithm, finding, searching, connecting and it says Nantucket, Nano technology, nangoli, Angelina Nangoli, and I erase, I delete, I go back and so I type NI and it goes Nicean, Nice, Night light, "Nightswimming" by REM. You like REM, right?

Nitrous oxide!

Nights of the round table!

Night lights! And I type NIG and it goes waaaaiiit a second.

[Slows down, starts backing up, hands slowly raising.]

Right?

[Smiling, eyebrows raised.]

Google's like, "Hey, I don't know about this . . ."

Google says, "I don't know if I like where *this* is going." [Looks out, smiles.] That's Google, ma'am, that is my impression of what Google is saying when I type NIG and I get ready to type another G . . . [Hesitant face, wincing, raising hand exaggeratedly over head, lowering it, pretending to type with gun on imaginary phone.] And Google's like, "Nope, uh-uh, no idea."

No idea, ma'am!

A blank stare! "Can't imagine where this is going," says Google!

Google is standing there, arms at side, kind of whistling and looking around.

It's playing dumb, Google has no idea where I'm going with this.

Google has no idea where I'm going with this NIG, ma'am? This is what we're supposed to believe? This is where we are?

That Google's all, "Doo doo doo, whistle whistle, what's that? NIG? Nope, no idea, lovely day, though . . ." [Pauses, looks out, menu face.]

Wait, nothing? Nothing? You have no idea.

Hmm? About what?

You have no idea. I type in NIG and you have nothing all of a sudden.

[Tight lips, shakes head stiffly.]

Hhmm mmm.

Nothing, not one thing. You were spitting out Nicean creed and nangoli a second ago.

But now, nothing? [Panicking, looking frantically, nervously side to side.] Nothing, ma'am, and I'm sweating now. [Wipes head, throws sweat at crowd, keeps pacing.] I'm wondering if any of this is real. Did I make this *up*, ma'am? Am I racist and don't even know it, ma'am? [Stops, looks out, hand slowly rising toward mouth.] Can that be, and oh my God, and nigger-toe-my-God, I'm thinking, am I a *racist*? Is this how you find out? [Looking up, out, into light, pleading.]

Because if I don't know *this* ma'am, that I'm a racist? [Pauses, smiles.] If I don't know this, what the hell else don't I know? And I think I can't think this and so I think fuck this, I have to finish, and I type, all caps, NIGGER . . . and nothing.

Nothing. Google is blank, it is white, and there is no sound, and it is so quiet. So I type T, and nothing, and hurry you have to hurry, finish this, because it is so close and it is all white and it is cold and O and E and S and there it is.

It says NIGGER TOES, I'm looking at it and I hit return and it's coming back up and what is the *first* thing it says, ma'am, the first thing that Google, your boy Google, comes back with, after all that, after all this?

BRAZIL NUTS!

SONOFABITCH, ma'am!

Are you fucking *kidding* me?

Top of the fucking page, plain as day. Brazil nuts. [Stops, exhales, laughs.] And of course it was, and I'm like why, Google? Why would you *do* that? Why did that have to happen? Why do we have to go through all of this when you knew what I was saying all along? Why did you have to make me think all that other stuff, that I was a racist? What's the point in that, in any of this?

[Looking up, looking out.]

And I shouldn't be *asking* that, should I? Like *that's not what I should be doing*, it sets a bad impression is what it does, and I've already said I don't do impressions, even though I've done like six already. [Smiles.] No, and I'm *saying* this now, *declaring* this, sir, *identifying*, and I've thought about it, I have, I've thought, oh no, this can't be happening. Like this can't be happening, any of this [Waving arms around, gesturing at room], any of this, this can't be happening, can it?

You ever feel like that, ma'am?

Do you kind of feel like that right now?

I get it. I get it, I do, and the only thing that makes sense?

And the only thing that makes sense is that it isn't. This isn't happening, sir. None of it, but that doesn't matter, I don't think. [Stands, stares, tired.] Here's something, and I'm just going to throw this out there, ma'am. Just sort of put it out there [Makes spreading motion with hands] on the table. I think my then-wife left because I didn't know what a cervix is. Not because of the Brazil nuts, ma'am. Not the bankruptcy, the drinking, the neglect, none of that, I don't think. I think it was the *cervix*, folks, the me not knowing what that was. I think that was what did it. The crux of this thing, ma'am, [Waves hands]. The crux of her exit, her cervexit, if you will. [Laughs, exhales.] I'm tired, ma'am. Imagine a table, ma'am. Then imagine that, the that that I just said, the cervix-that, on there, on that table.

And I'm going to level with you people, I don't know what a cervix is, and more importantly, I don't know when the best time to bring that up is. Is it now? Like at what point here tonight do we feel comfortable enough where I can say I don't know what a cervix is? Have we reached that level of familiarity yet? Has the appropriate amount of *time* passed? Has a rapport been established? Do we feel connected, are we there? I'm asking, here, because I don't know. About the cervix, the rapport, any of it. I'm lost, I declare. I mean, I know it's a thing, the cervix is, a thing that exists. I know there are such things as cervixes, you know, and I know that they're located in the vagina.

Lest you think, ma'am.

Contrary to popular belief, ma'am, and those are silly words, aren't they? Listen to that, listen to what I just said:

The cervix is located in the vagina.

[Makes confused face, grins. Shakes head.]

Listen to that, how can that possibly make sense, you know?

The cervix is located in the vagina.

Vagina.

Flo-flina.

Papaya.

These are words, these are words. I'm standing here making words, walking and talking on a stage. I'm declaring, I'm confessing, I'm atoning for whatever it is that I've done or haven't done, whichever, same thing. Nothing good can come from this, you know. [Looking down, looking distracted for a second then quickly looking up.] I know that a cervix is a thing and that it's a thing in the vagina, so my knowledge of it, I guess, is pretty limited. I don't know a lot about it, I don't know much.

[Looks up, looks down, looks out, eyes narrowed.]

You know that guy Aaron Neville, ma'am? He's a big, fat, I think Black guy? He's not really that Black, he's got a huge birthmark-looking thing on his face, and this really incongruous voice, like it's really high? Like he's this huge, enormous man and his voice is just so high and he sings that song and it goes, "I don't know much / but I know I love you / And that may be / all I need to know." You know that song, ma'am? And you notice how I said "huge and enormous" man instead of "morbidly obese man?" The nuances? Do you see the difference? Doesn't this speak to who I am, ma'am? A little bit about me, ma'am? My character and what have you? Shouldn't this be counted, shouldn't this count? The attention to detail, I declare? And is that a siren out there, a car horn, a foghorn and no, he doesn't know much, ma'am, this is admitted, we've admitted this, but *he does know he loves you* and *that* may be all he needs to know! [Stops, exhales dramatically. Bows to audience. Pauses, gathers himself.] No, I bet he would be a difficult guy to hang out with, Aaron Neville would. Like if you said, "Hey Aaron, do you know what time it is," he'd be like, "I don't know much, but I know I love you."

And you'd be like, "So is it five? Is it like five-thirty?"

[Crouching down, talking through clenched teeth.] And this is the part where I do my what-it-would-be-like-to-talk-to-Aaron Neville impression.

Aaron? [Looking around with a confused look] Do you happen to know where I put my keys?

I don't know much, but I . . .

Yeah, no, I know, I know. That's not, it's not helping me find my keys. Like I know you love me, but that's not helping. I got news for you. There's more that you need to know.

Aaron, what's the capital of New Hampshire?

Aaron, what's rack and pinion steering?

I don't know much . . .

Okay, we're done here, Aaron! We are done!

See, that to me, that would be difficult, right, ma'am? To hang out with Aaron Neville? And what were we talking about, cervixes? So I don't know a lot, I know it's a thing that exists in the vagina. The vagina of a woman, specifically. I know that, but I don't know a lot about it. My wife thought this was, I don't know, symbolic, I think. Indicative, I think. Of me being, I don't know, insensitive? [Looks out, shocked.]

Does that sound like me? Insensitive?

I know, what do I know? I know that an appendix is a thing. It's not in the vagina. And this isn't, don't think this is like a comprehensive list of all the things I know, ma'am. That's not fair. I'm making a comparison, is what I'm doing, with a word that sounds like another word. I'm giving an example of a word that I know the meaning of and comparing it to another word that sounds like that word that I don't know the meaning of. I don't know how this could be more clear. I'm saying that an appendix is a thing that serves some purpose in the body, except they really don't, because they are always bursting and being taken out of people. No, but why would I possibly know what a cervix is, specifically, like why would that ever come up? How is this relevant? Why in the world would I have to declare this? Who is tallying this, and how?

Chapter Ten
I Can't Explain

[Pauses. Stares out, stone-faced. Small smile breaks out across face.]

And I'm sorry, I am, but this is not good, is it? I mean, this isn't narrative progression, is it?

This is lovemaking?

This? It may be, I guess, in a loose definition of the word, maybe, but romantic?

Definitely not. No romantic lovemaking, no narrative progression, no goddamn closure. Only closure in here's *foreclosure*, ma'am, how about that? [Laughs, wipes brow with gun hand.]

And I shouldn't be having this conversation with you, should I? I mean, doesn't this subvert the whole, [Points gun at self then at audience] like there's a dynamic, here, right? Audience and speaker? Something? And no, and yeah, you can laugh, because it is funny, it really is. It's not something I ought to bring up, is it? But this is what this is now. This idea, my idea for this whole place? It's turned into this. Devolved, ma'am. Descended, ma'am, and think about that for a second, folks. [Walking slowly back and forth] And it's so quiet now and I'm talking softly, softly. Think about what that means. This whole thing was my idea. Renovating it was, building it was. An idea I had and was it a good idea? Jury's out, ma'am, jury's out. A different jury will probably be in soon. A hostage-taking jury, a multiple felony jury. *That* jury, ma'am, *those* juries have yet to convene. But regardless, but nevertheless, this is about the idea itself, the creation of a thing. Here's an idea I had one time. I'll go ahead and share this now, I mean, why not?

I've got an idea for a screenplay. [Eyes wide, smiling.]

I know!

Exciting!

No, but I've never really written a screenplay before, so I don't really know, you know, what's involved. The formatting, I've never done it, I don't know the proper form, I don't know what the fuck I'm talking about. I mean, come on. How would I write a play? All that direction? All that this goes here, that goes there? Too much, ma'am! Not a chance. I can barely pull *this* off, and I'm just fucking standing here, pretending like something is happening, or *has* happened, or is *about to* happen, some fucking thing. Time travel, am I right? [Shrugs shoulders, gives a whadda-you-gonna-do look.]

Anyway, here's my idea though, and I think it's a good one. This is what I've been working on. [Looks out, holds mic out to crowd.] Anybody here ever seen *Chinatown*? You know the movie *Chinatown*? Ma'am, *Chinatown*? Jack Nicholson? Sir, *Chinatown*? Should I say it again? *Chinatown*? [Nods, smiles.] This is banter, this is patter? Are those reindeer? Dashing and dancing? This is crowd work? *Chinatown*? You're familiar? Okay, good, good. We've got that. [Does that thing where you point at your own eyes and then point at the other person's eyes.] So this screenplay, my screenplay, [Pacing, excited] it's *exactly like Chinatown*, it's a retelling of *Chinatown*, except all the characters, the main characters, secondary characters, everybody, all of the characters are constantly throwing up.

[Eyes wide, expectantly.]

Hear me out.

It's just like *Chinatown*. Have you seen *Chinatown*? Ma'am?

You're looking at me like you may not have seen *Chinatown*.

Okay.

Imagine that, imagine *Chinatown*, the thing in your head and the thing in my head. Imagine that, except all the main characters are constantly vomiting. Like from the second the curtain goes up.

Or down, I don't know, does the curtain go up?

It goes up?

All right, then from when the curtain goes up, vomiting, it's just vomiting. They're all dressed the same, he's got the Band-Aid on his nose, you know? Right, there's a Faye Dunaway-type character, *she's* throwing up. Everybody's throwing up! What do you think?

It's challenging, I know, I get that. It's challenging for a couple of reasons. One reason is that I don't think that's been done. Like I don't know if you could do that. I don't know if anybody's done that. I mean, I don't know. I don't who know Bertolt Brecht is. I think he's somebody. Is Bertolt Brecht a person? That's somebody? I don't think in any of Bertolt Brecht's plays, you know? I don't think that he did that. You don't hear the name Bertold a lot, do you?

Who told?

*Ber*tolt.

That's something I'd say.

And is this going to be an evening of Bertolt Brecht conversations? Would *that* fit on the marquee? Do I think this is going to help my chances, here? Is that what I think? I told my then-wife this the other day, I forget when. I told her about my screenplay idea, I think. [Crouches down, whispering] This may or may not have happened, ma'am, I can't really say. This may be a fever dream, this may be the cancer talking, but I don't think it is, I think it happened, [Gets up, pacing] and when I *said this*, when I definitively and definitely *said this*, she didn't even roll her eyes at me, ma'am. Didn't even snort in

disgust, didn't say, "What the fuck are you talking about."
Nothing. And I guess that should have been a clue, a tell.
[Smiles.] She did eat a whole sleeve of Oreos, now that I
think about it. I wonder what that could mean. [Pauses,
laughs.]

What that means is this. Once upon a time, I thought
it would be a good idea to buy a building and renovate
it. It was a six-story building, still is, that hasn't changed.

You're sitting in that building right now.

I had to borrow a million dollars. This seemed like a
lot of money to me. I went to a bank. I said, "Would you
let me have a million dollars? I'll pay you back." [Stops,
looks out.] Do you know how tall six stories is, ma'am?
[Hunched over.] It's really tall, and I'm crouched down in
front of you, and I'm holding the mic in both hands. And
if it looks like I'm pleading, ma'am it's because maybe I
am. [Nodding slowly, standing back up, continues.]

Six stories is really tall and a million is a lot of dollars
and I was going to *buy this building* and turn it into a
movie theater. A movie theater that served food. And
showed films. I thought that would be a good idea, so I
did that and it was around then, right around then, that
I said to my then-wife, I said to her, "I'm not going to
explain myself."

And she looked at me like, "What do you mean by
that?"

She may have even said that. She may have even said,

"What do you mean by that?" and she may have been in the kitchen when she said that and I may have been in the doorway. I seem to recall standing in a lot of doorways during that period of time. Those were my standing-in-the-doorway years. And these are more like, as you can see, my walking-around years. My going bankrupt years. My dog dying years, my taking hostages years.

[Walking around, walking around.]

Anyway, that's something she may have said to me. And we can put that part on record, here. That's right, a part of this whole thing, this declaration.

An accounting, ma'am!

A reckoning, ma'am!

A tabulation, and she may have said, "What do you mean by that?" and maybe she did, ma'am, maybe she did, and even if she didn't? Even if I am making that up, if I am fabricating, if I am prevaricating, if there is a hint, a smidge, a tinge of fabrication and prevarication in this declaration, an eye of newt of it, ma'am, even if she didn't say that, she definitely *did* look at me like, "What do you mean by that."

That I know and I know that.

And that's a natural reaction, ma'am, it is. That makes sense. That is a natural thing to look like and even to say and I was so mad at her for looking and maybe saying that.

"What do I mean?"

"What do I *mean?*"

"I mean, I'm not gonna explain. I'm doing it right now, I'm doing it right now," I said, and these were real things that were said and eventually we were not married anymore, I was not living in that house, I did not own that movie theater, and none of that is the point.

The point is, things happen. The point is, there is no point in explaining that things happen. It doesn't make a difference, they're going to happen whether you explain them or not. I think I've made that pretty clear. Little bit about me, one time I thought I would buy a movie theater. One time I thought I would buy a dog-cobra. One time I thought I would write a screenplay. There was an old building in the town where I lived and live for now and in that building was an abandoned movie theater. I thought, "I am going to buy that building. I am going to buy that movie theater."

Two clear thoughts.

Look at them go.

When I decided I was going to do this, I'd ride my bike to it and look at it. It's very important, I think, that when I went to look at the building, I was on a bicycle. I was not a bike-riding guy back then, not a "cyclist." No padded shorts, ma'am, know nothing about helmets or tires. Can't think of any reason why I was doing that, why I would be riding a bike, but that is what I was doing, and it seemed very important at the time. Maybe it was, maybe it is. Maybe that was part of something. Riding my bike and looking at this building seemed to be a large part of how I was going to eventually get this building, and I know how this sounds, I do. The getting, I think I thought, would be directly tied into the riding and looking.

I would tell my then-wife that I was going to do this, that I was going to ride my bike down and look at the theater. I'm not sure she ever said anything about me doing this. I don't think she ever said anything like, "What?" or "You're doing what, now?" or "You have a bike?" Of course, any of these things would've been perfectly legitimate and reasonable things to say, perfectly legitimate and reasonable, any jury would agree.

Chapter Eleven

The Significance of a Dead Otter

Ladies and gentlemen of the jury, here are the facts. [Pacing, arms crossed behind back.] Several years ago, I decided to buy a movie theater. This is what I thought I would do back then and I have either said this before, or I will say it later, or I am saying it right now, doesn't matter, how could it? I do not understand time travel, your Honors, I am not an orgy guy. I was very famous in my town for this. For renovating the theater, not for not understanding time travel. That would be a strange thing to be famous for. Anyway, I bought a building, if it pleases the court. It used to be a movie theater, heretofore and forthwith. It was full of junk. In fact, let the record show there was so much junk, so much [Pauses, stage-whispers] so much shit, that you couldn't move. My brother and I saw a movie there once, *Superman 2*. Somebody stuck gum in my brother's hair. We were sitting in the balcony.

We were kneeling before Zod, and if it pleases the court, I bought that building and spent about a year knocking things down and cleaning things out. There were so many things in this building, your Honors. People would take pictures of me moving stuff out. I would lift things and throw things and tear things down. I did this for months and months. Everybody watched, the whole town did, and I'm going to stop here, for a second I think, because this isn't working. [Pausing, stopping. Hand with mic wiping forehead.] I mean, I am doing my best here. I am trying to explain, trying to declare. I am putting pieces together, fixing, sorting, and arranging. I am near the end, I am dying of cancer, I am declaring bankruptcy, the cops are at the door. I am wrapping up, people, and before I do, I am making sense of things, is what I'm doing, and you're all good people for bearing with me, you are. I appreciate you, I do. [Taps gun to chest, points out, nods.] You get me right here, for real. You're troopers, you're making the best out a bad situation. You're lemons and lemonade people, aren't you. You're just like me, all of you are. [Stops, stares. Smiles.]

You know.

[Smiles widely.]

The best frozen lemonade I ever had was at the Holocaust Museum. [Looks up.] What? Don't. Don't, and I'm serious, I'm getting tired. The best frozen lemonade I ever had was at the Holocaust Museum, for real.

This was in Washington DC, the nation's capital. Little clarification, folks, *the Holocaust Museum* is a museum designed to commemorate the victims of the Holocaust. Apt title!

For those of you who may not know, the *Holocaust* was a systematic, state-sponsored program of genocide in Germany where six million Jews were killed during World War II. Not World War II, The Dog, ma'am, the actual war. [Pauses, confused look on face.] I probably didn't need to clarify that, but anyway, *later* they built a museum to commemorate and honor, your Honors, the fallen. To remind us of the atrocities, to serve as a constant reminder of man's inhumanity towards man. They did this, they built that, and this *museum*, your Honors, it serves as a grim reminder of how awful we as a people can be. It's horrifying and it's real and it is a blatant, brutal reminder of what we are capable of.

It also serves great frozen lemonade.

And I don't know if these things are related at all, in fact I'm almost certain they aren't, but what do you think that means? You're a serious bunch. Like what do you think that means?

Because on the one hand, you've got a room full of shoes, right? That's all you hear about, is this room full of shoes. That's the big deal, that's what hits home, the shoes. The room full of them, the rooms full of them.

Sir, you seem to know what I'm saying, right?

What I'm doing?

I see your head nodding up and down. I see you nodding.

That's agreement, right?

That's what this is?

You're nodding in agreement? You're agreeing and we're nodding and we're doing this together? Good for you, sir, good for us. God bless.

So yeah, you go and you see all these shoes and it's horrifying and terrible, and you think how could people *do* this? How could they kill all these people, how could they slaughter them, how could they make *soap out of their fat*, ma'am! Which is a thing they did! They made soap out of the rendered fat of these brutally slaughtered people, and your mind is reeling, ma'am, with the horror and the terror and the sheer incomprehensibility of it all, but God *damn*, that frozen lemonade is good, you know?

It just is!

Why is it so goddamn good?

I don't know, ma'am I have no idea! And you feel *guilty* now, don't you, ma'am? For just *hearing* this, and you're sitting there, there's this room full of shoes, there's six million dead, and you're sitting there, [Pretends mic is a straw, makes loud slurping noise] sucking down a fucking lemonade? The fuck is *that*, you know? I declare! [Stops, deadpans.] No, but seriously, the frozen lemonade, how does that fit in, right? Because it has to go somewhere, right? This is something I should be declaring, right? Because if it isn't . . . it's just poor taste, right, ma'am? [Hunching, scrunching.] If it doesn't fit, I mean. Like this, like if I said the best Bananas Foster I ever had was at the Holocaust Museum, then *that*, yes, abso-LUTELY that would be in bad taste!

Because of the burning, ma'am, the incinerating, sir!

But this is in *good* taste, ma'am, so this all has to go somewhere, so I *guess where this goes*, is that when I was at Butler University, my friend who looks Jewish but isn't and I went to this movie theater. It served food and drinks, alcoholic drinks. This was something back then, not something like it is now. Back then it was something, ma'am, and now? [Shrugs.] It's something. Anyway, when I was there I got a drink. It was called a Jack Frost. It was Jack Daniels and frozen lemonade. It probably still is, isn't it? I mean, the drink is still called that right, that hasn't changed? Ma'am, are you sitting here trying to tell me that the drink I remember as a Jack Frost, *clearly* as a Jack Frost, that that drink isn't called that anymore? A Jack Frost is not that drink? Or that drink is no longer called a Jack Frost? Which? Which is it that you're saying? [Laughing.] And that was my impression of a guy getting indignant that the name of a drink he once had may or may not have changed.

I'm digging deep tonight people.

Anyway, that drink was delicious, the one I had at

the movie theater in Indianapolis. Was it better than the one at the Holocaust Museum? That's a great question, ma'am, a great question.

But let me ask you. [Pauses.]

Six million.

What does that even *mean*, six million?

I could keep saying it, I could keep asking. Six million? Ahem.

Are you getting tired of this? Me too, and we've got to be wrapping up soon, right? Where the hell are these cops, already? This is almost over. It's exhausting and it's enough. Do I have anything else to declare, anything else before the cops come in, before they bust down my battened hatches? Anything before I die alone of cancer? Anything? Let's see, let's see. [Pinches bridge of nose, exhales. Looks up, menu-faces.] Maybe?

Maybe this is important? I mean this *seems* like it's important. It's about otters and hang on, no, this is good, this means something. There's a lot of, right, a lot of connections, and similarities and things that will make this relatable, things that will help discern the narrative or something, I think, you tell me.

Last weekend at the zoo, all the lemurs were throwing up. [Shakes head real quick.] I know lemurs are not otters, but hear me out. All of them, all the lemurs, all at the same time, were throwing up. I saw this and I thought to myself and maybe out loud, I thought: so many lemurs, so much throwing up.

There could have been ten of them, ten lemurs, ten lemurs at the zoo, at my zoo, at the zoo in the town where I live.

Ma'am, a lemur is a monkey.

Sir, you know what ten is.

Anyway, most of my entire family was watching them. My then-wife and I and our six boys were there. We were standing there, looking at lemurs, watching lemurs, look at them go.

The whole family, the whole zoo. We were standing in the monkey house, just standing there looking at the monkeys. There are worse things.

Then we heard a sound.

A wet sound, a wet slapping sound.

A sound like soup, buckets of soup dumped, being slapped, being wet. Hot soup, wet soup, splashed soup.

So we looked, all of us, looked at the lemurs, and the lemurs were throwing up. It was like a lemur *Chinatown*. We watched them do this, all of us, because what else were we going to do? Were we going to *not* watch the lemurs throw up? Is that what you're suggesting, sir? [Frown, small shake of head.] Don't be ridiculous. No, we watched. We watched the lemurs throw up, and I know I said I don't do impressions, but it was like:

BLAAAH!

COUGH!

They made sounds like *CARTOON!*

And I pointed and made a sound like *AAAH!*

One of my boys pointed and made a sound like *EWWW!*

After the lemurs made their sounds and my family made their sounds, I said, "There must be something wrong with these monkeys." Real calmly, very matter-of-fact. [Looks out in audience as an aside.] It's about delivery, ma'am, this whole thing is.

And I'm envisioning a lemur who has just finished retching and heaving and slip-slapping soup out of his monkey mouth, ma'am, his lemur mouth. I envision this lemur wiping remnants of vomit off of his furry mouth with the back of his furry hand and hearing me say this, hearing me say, "There's something wrong with these monkeys," and looking up at me and being like, yeah. His monkey eyes would be red from the throwing up. He'd blow some monkey air out his monkey nostrils and give a tiny monkey snort.

He'd be like, "You ain't kidding."

He'd be like, "I hear *that.*"

He'd nod at me when he said this, a small lemur nod, some small lemur understanding. I said this out loud, said what I just said just now, about the monkey hearing me and responding like that.

My boys laughed.

My then-wife did not. She did not react at all. Nothing, ma'am, zero, not a thing. Not a snort, not an eye-roll, not an Oreo-eat, and does that sound *right?*

When ten lemurs all start vomiting at the same time? And here's a little bit about me, ma'am. If I'm at the zoo? And even *one* lemur throws up? I'm talking about it for days. I'm telling everybody I know, and I'm telling them more than once.

"How was your weekend?"

"I SAW A LEMUR THROW UP!"

And that may be an exaggeration, but I really don't think it is. That seems like something notable, something worthy of a reaction. But ten lemurs? Good lord, ma'am. [Mouth open, eyes wide, stunned and shocked.] Where to *begin?* I mean, that seems like something, doesn't it? That would elicit a reaction? This is my then-wife, people, the then-mother of my then-kids, and there are ten lemurs vomiting, we are witnessing this, we all are, and she is acting like nothing is happening. [Shakes head, menu-faces at nothing. Wipes tears from eyes.]

This is all making more and more sense, but that's not what this is about. This is about now, and now is about zoos, now is about otters. This an evening of romantic lovemaking, this is me establishing rapport. These are connections being made. A throughline, this is discernible narrative progression. We can trace this, you and I can, we can see how the lemur vomiting and the otter dying and the theater dying has led to this point. It is an exercise in inevitability, ma'am. When ten lemurs vomit simultaneously, ma'am? Die are cast, ma'am. Gauntlets thrown, but we're not here to talk about dice and gauntlets, are we ma'am? We're here to talk about dead otters.

The otter, whose name was Chloe, died at the zoo, in the town where I live and where those lemurs threw up in front of my boys and then-wife. So that earlier story? That was just setting the stage, the lemur-vomiting was. That was me setting the tone. But this particular otter dying meant a lot to me.

And I know what you're saying. You're saying, "Otters die."

You're saying, "They die all the time, every day."

You're saying, "That's life."

You're saying this kind of softly, kind of quietly.

You're kind of wincing when you say this.

You're wondering if I get it, if I understand this.

You're watching me standing here looking at you.

You're wondering if I can see you.

You are feeling sorry for me.

You're saying, "Otters die," and you've said that twice now.

You're saying, "An otter died right now, just now, right in front me, right while you were saying that last thing."

You are holding this dead otter up right now.

You are standing up.

You are waving it in my face.

You are angry.

"This otter is dead!"

You are screaming.

"Why don't you grow up? Let us out of here, you asshole!" you are screaming, and I hear this and I know and I agree. There's nothing I can do about it though, I don't think. This is the world we live in, we live in a world where otters die, where people declare things and where people leave and get taken hostage and it would be stupid and silly of me not to admit this, and I know this, so you can all just sit back down.

[Looks up, timidly. Eyes wide. Expectant. Hesitant.]

Earlier tonight, I said something about how I was on TV all the time back then, right? Back when I first started renovating this? Sir, I said that, didn't I? Always on TV, always on the radio, the papers. This happened, right? [Looks out, panicked.] It did? Oh, thank God. Again, not great at time travel, so bear with me, but no, "Look at him go!" they said. "He loves it!"

[Crouches down, whispers.] Little bit about me, ma'am, I did not love it! At all!

I hated it!

I was so scared, ma'am! What was I *doing?* I had no idea! None, I'm just in there with the shit and the rubble and the maybe carburetors. Cleaning it out, making a path. And then when it was done? When it was open and the theater was going?

Same thing.

TV, radio.

"Look at this!" "So happy!" And meantime, I am
dying, ma'am. Dying from the cancer, the histoplasmosis. I am dying from all of it, from everything, and
what, ma'am, what does this have to do with an *otter*?
But before I get into that, you know what'd be really cool
now? No, this is good, this is good, it'd be cool if a camera was to pan out and slowly, slowly come into focus on
this mess, right? This huge mess with stuff everywhere,
and it's like I'm on stage and you're out there and I'm
talking and walking around and it's panning out, right?
And you can see it all, and all of this mess is strewn about,
boxes and garbage and rubble and maybe carburetors,
and we're there, and it's in the middle of all this mess,
all this majesty and it pans out, and it gets higher and
higher, you can see lights flashing outside, the red lights,
and the red light from the police car mixes with the light
from the spotlight, the one that's on me, and I'm there,
there in all that light, and we're all together. Wouldn't
that be cool, ma'am? And I can do this, I can explain it,
I can, I declare! It is like this, good people. [Wipes tears
from eyes, clears throat.] Once upon a time, there was
an otter named Chloe. Chloe the Otter, they called her,
I'm imagining, and she became quite a big deal. You see,
ma'am, Chloe was not any old otter. She was pregnant!
Pregnant with tiny otter babies!

Oh my lord, ma'am!

Hand to forehead, ma'am! [Puts hand to forehead.]

What is cuter than *that*?

Nothing!

That is *it*, that's the cutest thing there is. Empirically, ma'am! Quantifiably, sir, I declare. So we were all excited, right? Whole town was. The zookeepers, the newspaper people, me, you, everybody. Good lord, we were about to have a bunch of slippery, fuzzy otter babies rolling around all over the goddamn place!

Exciting!

Chloe the Otter was on the front page! There she is, big belly, staring contentedly at the camera. Posing, proud, expectant. Full of promise, right? Can you see it? Can you see her there? Everybody knows what an otter is, ma'am. An otter is not a cat. And there was a webcam, too! A webcam, ma'am!

To document, to preserve! We don't want to miss a minute, and there she was, remember? Slipping and sliding? *Cavorting*, ma'am, I think the word is. I think the word is *cavorting*. Like if we were describing, ma'am? If I was to try and describe what Chloe was doing, I think *cavorting* is an apt, you know, description, but anyway, there she was, romping and cavorting and generally endearing herself to our community. Every now and again she'd kind of look at the camera, and flick her whiskers, you know? Take a paw, and kind of brush her fur back off of her eyes, and say something witty. Something like, "Well, my wife'll be glad when I'm done so I can

start working on *our* house!" She was something else, she
was, she was, but there was only one problem, ma'am,
a *tiny* hitch in the story. It turns out, Chloe died. Yeah,
she did, she died. Big story in the news. "Otter Dies" or
something like that, I don't know. I'm guessing. "Dead
Otter!" Something like . . . what's that? [Cups hand to
ear, listening.]

An audible gasp?

Is that what that was?

You're probably wondering what happened to the
babies, right? These little orphaned otters? The sun's *not*
gonna come out, otters, not tomorrow, not any day, and
do you know *why*, ma'am?

[Pause, shakes head.]

Tumors!

Not babies, sir, not adorable, empirical baby otters!

Tumors!

Cancerous tumors! The worst kind of tumors!

See, and plot twist, Chloe was never pregnant! Her
belly *wasn't* full of babies, far from it, sir!

Not babies, tumors!

It was full of tumors!

Tumors that were killing her!

And we laughed, didn't we?

We laughed when we saw her, belly fat, slipping and
sliding around! All those plaintive looks in the camera, all
those fun interviews, that whole time, what she was really

saying was, "Why isn't anybody helping me? I am dying."

When she said stuff like "I sure do love eating fish," what she was really saying was, "I am dying. Rotting from the inside. Please help me."

When she said, "I hope these kids like selling popcorn," she was really saying, "I am scared and I don't know what I am doing." And this is far from where we started, I get that, but I can't help but think this is important, you know? What does *this* have to do with romantic lovemaking, ma'am? I mean, nothing? Dead otters and lemurs puking? Not, ah, not the most romantic thing I can think of, but it's something, isn't it? Something I should declare, to you, to me, to somebody.

Chapter Twelve
We're All Wrong

This makes complete sense, and we're wrapping up here, we are, I promise. So, in summary, so to wrap up, to declare, finally and definitively what is going on here, let me make one last statement. When I was going bankrupt after I started my movie theater, I had to *declare* bankruptcy, which was funny to me. Not that it was happening, ma'am, *not* that, but like why do you have to *declare* bankruptcy? To *declare it?* I don't know, doesn't that seem a little much?

Like, you know, if I *mention* it? That's one thing. If it comes up in conversation, in passing, fine, but I don't think this will be something I'd want to *declare*. Like what do you *declare*, sir? What constitutes, you know? What is the criteria? I mean, I started this whole thing here, that's something, right? Married, helped raise a couple of kids. I would declare *that*, that would be something I would

declare, but this? That I failed? That I have cancer? That
I am a failure, a hostage-taker? That I'm not an orgy guy?
That I know what Brazil nuts are, this is important? Any
of this is important? Any of this change anything? No,
and I had to declare bankruptcy, had to go and do it, and
when the day came, I struggled a lot, as you can imagine. Like what to wear. I mean, what do you wear to a
bankruptcy hearing. How do you dress for this, for that?

Do you dress up?

Do you, like, wear a shirt and tie, stuff like that? Is
that business casual, ma'am? Is it business business? Is *that*
a thing? Do you do *that*? Or do you, you know, wear a
nice pair of jeans and a blazer? Like maybe a blazer and
a pair of jeans, something like that? I've always thought
I could pull off that look, ma'am. That's a little bit about
me right there, right there at the end. But no, do you
wear a barrel with suspenders? You know, like a huge
pickle barrel or something and nothing else? Whatever,
I go to the courthouse, and I *think* I wore a shirt and tie
because, you know, why not? Why not, how many times
are you going to do this? I hope just once. And yeah, and
yes, and I know that I said that this hasn't happened yet,
right? I know I've said, "Oh, tomorrow I'm going to do
this and that and that's why you're all here," right? And
I'm like, "There are bombs on the doors" and "Plastique"
and all that shit, right? But let's be honest, that was just
narrative progression, right? That was hemming and that

was hawing, but that's not the point, the point is *what do you wear* to a bankruptcy, and you know the worst-case scenario? The worst-case scenario is, I dress up and I'm the only one there in a shirt and tie. But even that is not the worst thing in the world, is it, ma'am? So, I'm there with a bunch of people in this room, this courtroom in Bloomington, Illinois, the town I live in. I was in the courthouse in a courtroom and there was a bunch of people there. We were all getting ready to declare. We were all there together. There was a woman sitting across from me holding her phone and yelling. The phone had a tiger-striped case and her face looked like every face you have ever seen, ever. She was yelling, but she didn't sound angry. This was the first thing I noticed, how she didn't really sound angry, even though she was yelling. She was talking about the Tarantino movie that was about Clint Eastwood and the car.

"No, it *was* him," she yelled into her tiger phone. "I just *saw* it, Cheryl. I think I'd know." She was sitting next to an obese woman wearing what appeared to be a child-sized T-shirt. The shirt was black. It had a heart on it, a bedazzled heart, and right in the middle, it said "Me So Spicy."

[Stares into crowd.]

I had no idea what this meant.

It meant something I didn't understand. Fat was bulging out the be-jewels. I could see her belly hanging over her jeans. We all could. This was a decision she'd made, wearing the Me So Spicy shirt to her bankruptcy hearing. A decision like wearing the shirt and tie was for me. Like holding you hostage, like bombs, like doors. Like things in boxes. I thought some more. I thought how the decision had been made to *buy* that shirt, to *make* the shirt. I thought how far back it went, I thought what it meant, and decided I didn't know, because it didn't matter, not then it didn't. Then, we were all there for the same reason. And there were other people in there, sure there were, and I could go on and on, and if I were better at this I would, but this was enough, I think and thought then. The yelling woman said something to I guess Cheryl about a Toronado and Me So Spicy exhaled loudly and leaned back farther into her seat and I realized why I was really here.

I was wrong.

I was there because I was wrong.

I'm wrong, the lady's wrong, Me So Spicy's wrong. We're all wrong, we've done wrong things, and now we're trying to get right. We were wrong, and now we're trying to fit everything in. We were wrong and we have to confess. We have to declare. I liked this. This made sense. I may have smiled.

We're trying to reconcile.

To settle the books and say this is it. We're trying to say and from here on out. And we are resolving and we

are declaring, all of us are, because we were wrong, and
we have to admit, in public, in front of everybody. We
have to *declare* that we fucked up, made mistakes, were
wrong.

This is simple, I thought.

I am getting ready to do this, I thought. I am ready to
do this, I thought, and before I could go up and confess
and declare my bankruptcy, they called somebody else up.

Gary.

Anyway, so yeah, so this is Gary, one of us, and what
they did was they called everybody up individually, and
they did the same thing with everybody. You had to state
your name and all this other stuff. Who you were, where
you lived. So they called this guy up, Gary Something.
And Gary came to the front, and he was an average looking middle-aged fellow. Dark hair, maybe a mustache.
Maybe a shirt with sharks on it, maybe a cartoon mask,
a Fred or Barney mask. Maybe a Viking helmet, and
ma'am, I'm going to be honest here, I have no idea what
he looked like. None. I can't remember it at all. He was
vanilla, Gary was. He could have been the woman with
the tiger phone, could have been Me So Spicy, he could've
been someone else entirely, doesn't matter, how could it?
Anyway, Gary went up there and there was another guy
with him, with Gary. And they asked Gary his name, and
he said Gaawwee.

Gaawwee.

Like that. And they asked his address and he said something like Eeeweven Twewve One Too Fwee Stweet or something, like that, with those wet, slapping sounds. You know how deaf people talk? I SAID DO YOU KNOW HOW DEAF PEOPLE TALK? [Laughs.] It's Okay, ma'am, we're all having fun. [Leans in, whispers.] He's not here, and he couldn't hear us anyway. He's deaf. [Stands up, keeps walking.] Okay, but yeah, that's how he talked, Gaawee. He even *talked* wrong, is what I'm saying and have just said. So Gary told them his address—One Too Fwee, whatever—and the guy next to him goes, no, that's not right. No, that's not right, the guy says and then he goes and gives a completely different address, 43 Bricklebaw or something. Nothing like One Too Fwee any-fing. And then the judge asked for his phone number, for Gary's phone number and Gary said something and the guy next to him says, "No, sorry your Honor. His phone number is . . ." Then Gary talked about some other things, the judge or whoever, was it a judge? I don't know for sure, I think maybe it was, but whoever it was asked Gary more questions and Gary answered them with his flat, wet words and the guy *next* to Gary calmly corrected every one of his answers. And this took I don't know how long, and all the time Gary was up there being wrong was more time I would have to spend being wrong, and I would've been upset, but I knew it didn't matter, my turn was coming soon. Soon I would declare.

Reconciliation, I thought.

Settling, I thought.

A righting of wrongs, I thought.

I thought of Tiger Phone. I thought of Me So Spicy. I thought our time is coming. I thought we'd have to wait just a little longer because Gary was wrong about everything, every single thing, just like we all were. Gary was wrong, I was wrong, all of us were wrong, differently, the same. We're all the same, I was thinking, and I was surprisingly Okay with this and I was smiling and I was thinking I get it.

Because I did.

Epilogue
We Can Say This Out Loud

And that sounds great, doesn't it? And we could end right there, couldn't we, ma'am? With this scene, and cut, and wrap, and print. And that would be it, ma'am, and it would be in the can, ma'am [Quick shake of head, little smile], and I apologize, and no, that's not what I meant, ma'am, not at all. One last joke I guess, one last thing to ruin everything. I'm sorry, I really am, but no, and I'd walk out of there, out of that courtroom, and I'd kind of look up, you know? You know how you kind of look up, ma'am? You just look out at the bright crisp afternoon, just kind of menu-face up at the sky, you know? Just kind of squint into the bright sunlight, the bright sunshine that came just out of nowhere but had been there the whole time? You know how that is ma'am [Crouching down, slumping forward], when it's like the thing you're looking for, the thing you always needed and wanted even though you didn't know you always needed or wanted it, whatever that is, who cares, when *that* thing is like right in front of you the whole time? [Looks out, pleading.] And you're kind of like *huh*, you know? Sir, you know how you're sometimes kind of like *huh*? And I'm pleading, sir. And I'm asking, ma'am, and you know how that is? And wouldn't that be *great*? That would be a scene, wouldn't it? That would be something, it would, it would. [Stands still, looking out. Blinking back tears.]

And it's so quiet, isn't it?

That's the scene where it's quiet, but there's another scene where it's so loud and everything falls down. All of this. It comes crashing down, all of it does, everything that was here. It blows up, it explodes and everything crashes down. Everything that I took out and everything I put back in. All of it was back, all of it never left, and it collapses on top of me. [Stops, smirks.]

On top of me?

A top of me? Does that, is that, and I know, and this is serious and I'm sorry, and I will do this again, I will try this again. I am sorry, I have cancer.

I am sorry, I am alone.

I am sorry, this is all over.

This will be better, I promise you, ma'am, just don't leave. [Deep breath, squaring shoulders.]

There is a scene where everything falls down.

All of it.

It comes crashing down, all of it.

All of the things that were there and all of the things that I put there. All of it is back, all of it never left, and it falls on me, collapses on me. I am consumed and subsumed, it is everywhere, and everywhere. Rubble and shards and jagged edges. Dust and silt and in the ears and lungs. I choke, I cough, I cannot breathe. It is in my lungs, coating and corroding. Even if I got out, I think. Even if we get out, even if we were ever even here, and I am thinking this as the walls come down, as they blow up, as they explode. As doors are stormed. Even if I get out, this is already in me and it will never go away, never. This dust, this residue, this smoke. This film on lungs. Coating and corroding, sir. Permeating, ma'am. It's all that I have left, and I am sorry, I am so sorry.

But that's no way to end it, is it?

Like this?

That is no scene, ma'am, that is no scene, sir!

That is not worth the price of admission. We don't want that, we want closure, and this is that, and there is a scene, and he drives home. He drives home and he pulls into his garage and before he even gets out of the car, his wife is standing there at the window. He can see her. She is looking at him.

Oh, this is nice.

She comes to him, she does, his then-wife does. His then-and-now wife does, eyes expectant, eyes full of tears,

tears and a quiet finality and she looks at him through the glass, and he's about to say something, to declare something and she says shush.

Oh, this is so nice, this is why we are here, isn't it?

This is what this is.

This is intimate, this is romantic lovemaking, it is so quiet.

Shush, she says and he is so tired and it is all finally over and he quietly weeps. They are together and they are weeping and it is over. It is all over, I declare, and he's exhausted and it is over and he is in love and she is in love and the boys, ma'am? The beautiful boys, they walk in and can you see this, ma'am? And this is over now, isn't it? They are here now, aren't they? And are they in blue? And we can't see through all the smoke, can we sir, but I will tell you, and I declare.

It is like this.

The boys see mom and dad crying and they say dad are you crying. And you are so you say you are. And they say why and you look around. You look at your wife and your boys. You can see them through the smoke and the sirens and the pounding on the doors, it's just them, that's all you can see. You see them pounding at the doors, pounding at the glass. Bigger than a building, bigger than anything else, and you say because of this. You say I'm crying because I built all of this.

CPSIA information can be obtained
at www.ICGtesting.com
Printed in the USA
JSHW021118090123
35924JS00003B/5